H.E. Lewis is the author of a previous novel,
House Rules, and is working on a new novel featuring
Detective Caroline Reese. She lives in New York City.

Praise for H.E. Lewis and *The Second Suspect*:

"Shocking, vicious and disturbingly dark"
Publishing News

"an electrifying novel"
Family Circle

"A devastating look at the nature of power and control,
particularly when it involves men and money"
San Francisco Chronicle

"This disturbing tale of a protected sociopath packs a
frisson on every page"
Publishers Weekly

"Fast paced, suspenseful and deliciously dark"
Out

"A skin prickling story full of strange surprises"
Library Journal

Also by H.E. Lewis

House Rules

The Second Suspect

H.E. Lewis

PIATKUS

To the memory of my mother
EDITH MILLER LEWIS
1919–1996

MONDAY

One   Afterwards, Ingrid drew the girl a bath. She put oil in it, oil she'd brought from home because, even after all these years, she could still convince herself that her husband brought her to beautiful hotels for normal reasons.

She spent a good deal of time making sure the water was warm but not hot, that the bath was pleasurably full. Then she carefully laid towels—large, soft, white hotel towels—on a small satin-covered bench that stood opposite the sink.

What remained was to carry the girl to the tub. She hadn't asked her husband for help with this. It wasn't something he'd understand. And, of course, he had his own errands. She hoped she could finish with this before he returned. That he wouldn't spoil this, too.

Carrying the girl took less effort than Ingrid had imagined it would. She was neither a young woman nor a strong one, and so the ease of this added to her belief that she was doing the right thing. It wasn't until she'd gotten her into the tub that things went wrong again.

She began to work the knots. She'd thought the water would make this easier, but the oil had been a mistake. Her fingers slipped on her husband's leather belt. Looped through its buckle, it cinched the girl's neck. And this thin leather band only pulled tighter as Ingrid tried to loosen it, as she tried to free the girl's wrists, which were tied behind her back.

Ingrid had to turn her, but this forced the girl's face into the water. So Ingrid worked the leather in the dark because she'd needed to close her eyes to this.

Gabriel Santerre walked calmly to the nearest sporting-goods store. He stood before racks of golf clubs, testing grips, feigning his swing. He waited to be served.

When the salesman approached, Santerre smiled. He still held one of the clubs as he made his request. "I'd like you to show me some travel cases," he said. "Large ones."

The clerk, not some youngster but a man in his late fifties, Santerre's age, wore a suit. It was that type of store. He said, "We have some hard-shell cases. Very protective. Easy to carry."

Santerre pretended to consider this. He returned the club to the rack, nodding his head. "Lead away," he said.

The two went to the back of the store. Once there, the clerk pulled cases, one after another, from a display. Santerre inspected each one carefully, still with a slight smile on his face. He ran his fingers over grainy plastic, smoothed velveteen interiors, snapped latches.

Handing the last one back, testing the weight as he did, Santerre said, "I suppose I'm old-fashioned. Why don't you show me something in leather. Or vinyl perhaps is lighter."

"Of course," the clerk said, bending to slide open a wooden door beneath the display. He pulled out a case, one stacked atop others wrapped in plastic.

Santerre took it from him, shaking it a little before holding it lengthwise. He did this to loosen the crease it bore from being stored folded over. Now extended, the case reached his chest while touching the floor. Satisfied with this, he tested the zipper—wide, sturdy metal—running nearly to the bottom and then over the head where it stopped.

He inspected the closure meticulously. The stitching was reinforced with rivets, securing a metal plate beneath the fabric. A small padlock was provided to lock the zipper—too flimsy to keep anyone out, but at least enough to discourage a casual glance inside, enough to keep the zipper from simply slipping open.

He upended the case and found the same sort of metal plate at the base of the zipper. It convinced him that this bag would serve his purpose.

"Yes," he said, handing it back to the clerk.

"And the color, sir?"

"What?" Santerre asked.

"Color. Do you have a preference?"

"Ah, what are my choices?"

"Black, of course. There's also a handsome dark green, navy, burgundy. Oh, and a turquoise. More for the ladies, but easy to spot at baggage claim."

"Burgundy, I think."

The clerk knelt beside the sliding door, searching through the stack and retrieving the desired color. He then gently refolded the sample, replaced it, and closed the display case.

Together they walked to the front of the store. Santerre paid in cash, naturally. The clerk put the purchase into a bag. The two exchanged thank-yous, and then Gabriel Santerre was out on the street, walking back to the hotel.

Santerre returned to their suite still pleased by his excursion. But what he found upon opening the door and glancing around did not please him. The place was in disarray. Their things were not packed. But he found the real disorder when he opened the bathroom door.

Ingrid was slumped between the tub and the wall, barely dressed, hair in tangles, her face blotched with lipstick smears, makeup smears, her eyes looking like she might've cried before becoming this listless.

The girl was a soggy mess in the tub. Mostly naked, leaning in a corner. Her neck and head above water, letting the leather dry and constrict. Her flesh on either side swelling. There was an unpleasant odor. All this would make things more difficult.

Santerre pulled the tub's stopper, an old-fashioned one attached to a chain. While he waited for that water to drain, he ran more water into the sink, steaming water. Then he took a washcloth from the towel rack and doused it.

"Clean yourself," he said, throwing it at his wife.

It hit Ingrid's face, clung to her cheek for an instant before dropping into her lap. She still didn't move. If Santerre had cared to look he would've seen dreamy eyes—open, but not to anything in this room.

"I can see you're going to be no help," he said, "no help at all." And then he left her.

In the other room he took off his jacket, hanging it on the back of a chair. He removed his tie, cuff links, and then his shirt. Lastly, he dropped his watch into the ashtray with his cuff links. He fingered the chain around his neck, then the glass bauble suspended from it, but, as always, he kept the necklace on.

He returned to the bathroom in just his undershirt, suit pants, socks, and shoes. If Ingrid could've seen at all, she would've noticed the disgust on his face, forced as he was to kneel down and pick up the girl, slimy still from the oil and water. He carried her to the bed, laying her down beside the golfing case, still in its plastic wrapper.

Maybe the absence of the girl stirred Ingrid because now she stood in the doorway, looking at her husband. "I've called the police," she said.

"No you haven't."

And it was true. She'd thought to, but she hadn't actually done it. She might've been able before she put the girl into the tub. She might've had the strength to, then. But then she had still believed things were all right, that she could make them all right, and this had canceled the need to call for help.

But by the time the girl was in the tub, by the time Ingrid closed her eyes to her while working the knots in oily water, by then the need for help was so acute it became unactionable. And so Ingrid resorted, as she usually did when under this type of strain, to dreaming. A dreaming that let her eyes open again but see nothing of her immediate surroundings.

Gabriel Santerre set to work. He walked right past Ingrid, back to the bathroom for a towel. He wiped his hands with it as he crossed the room again to the bed. His hands clean now, he put one into his pants pocket and took out a small penknife. He opened it and began sawing through belt leather.

"Well, you've ruined this," he said, meaning only the belt. "Look at it."

These last words he said more to himself. He'd cut the belt in half and this allowed him to free it from the girl's neck. Her hands stayed caught by the knot Ingrid had been unable to loosen. He worked the blade under the knot with deliberate movements. He would not accidentally cut her. He would not abide having to clean up blood.

Ingrid had moved to the phone. Her eyes stayed fixed on him and so she touched the keys blindly, unsure even of how to get an outside line. And though her eyes never left him, not for a moment, he still managed to surprise her, coming across the room very fast, yet not seeming to hurry.

This still didn't seem to have happened even when the receiver was not in her hand anymore but in his. She heard it crack against her jaw. Heard the blow that sent her to the floor but never felt it. Not even when her hand went mechanically to her face, rubbing the soreness she had yet to feel.

"Oh, please," he said.

He returned to the bed. Took up his knife again. His hands stayed steady as he finally freed the girl's. Now, he gathered up the pieces of the belt. Laid them on the bed beside her. He wiped the blade on the towel before using it to open the golfing case wrapper. Then he closed the knife and put it back into his pocket.

Ingrid remained on the floor through all this. She was sitting now, her arms curled around her knees. She had nothing to lean on where she was. Her head ducked under the table that held the phone. She rocked slightly in a familiar, comforting motion. She'd gone back dreamy, vacant.

Santerre shook the case from its wrapper. He put the belt pieces into the now empty plastic. Folded the plastic over several times, rolled it.

His annoyance at the belt was not simply a question of waste, though certainly that was a part of it. He derived pleasure from wearing belts he'd used in this fashion. He had worn this same one for several years, seven years actually. But because he'd cared for it well, it didn't appear shabby. This was the thing he'd oiled and cleaned.

He carried it across the room. Set it on the table his wife still sat beneath. Then he returned to the bed. Turned his attention to the case, smoothing its fold, opening the zipper.

The sound of this jarred Ingrid—a harsh, biting sound too loud for her to defend against. Her eyes widened, seeing movements in a blur, but seeing them, unable not to.

There was the girl. Her husband. The case. Him rolling the girl into the case. A motion that made Ingrid's head swim first and then her stomach. She wanted to get up. She tried to but instead found herself rolling. Lying on the floor now instead of sitting, though still curled in a similar way.

Just as she began to dream the sound happened again. Longer this time, in halting, jerky bites. Her teeth scraped against each other, making another unsettling noise, and then her husband's breathing intruded, too. She wanted to cover her ears but couldn't loosen her hands from her knees.

The sound stopped then. Now there was only her husband and the case. Him lifting it from the bed, placing it on the floor near the door.

"Get yourself dressed," he said. "See if you can make yourself presentable."

The first step to this would've been washing her face, but he'd taken a clean undershirt into the bathroom, was running water in there. She got to her feet and, on standing, felt an aching in her jaw. This reminded her of the phone. The water was still running. She lifted the receiver. If she could behave the way he did, do things precisely for just a short time. Do this one thing well, everything would change.

She touched the keys carefully this time, following the instructions right there on the phone. She heard a voice on the other end, then her own, saying very simply, "There's been a murder."

She gave the hotel name, their name, and, after answering questions, she returned the receiver to the cradle, went back down under. Under the table, under the water still running in the bathroom. She curled there again, on the floor, wondering if she'd done what she believed she had or merely imagined again.

Two   Detective Caroline Reese had spent this Monday morning on the phone, trying to track down witnesses to a random shooting on Central Park South. Getting nowhere with this, she welcomed her lieutenant calling her into his office.

As he closed the door, she felt the familiar tingle of something big brewing, and about to be handed to her. Lieutenant Harris spoke hurriedly, in a hushed, almost conspiratorial fashion.

"Got something for you," he began.

Reese nodded, waiting for more.

"We just got a call from the Ascot Towers. You heard of the Santerres?"

"Vaguely. Don't spend much time on the society page."

"Well, a woman called 911. Said there'd been a murder over there. Said her name was Santerre. That's all it took for bells and whistles to start ringing—uptown and downtown. You with me?"

"Uh-huh."

"So I need you and Miller to get over there fast. You're to bring the wife in. Let the others grab the husband, but you stick close to the wife."

"Got it."

"Reese . . ."

"Yeah."

"You know what you're looking for?"

"Got some idea."

"Grab her fast. Separate her."

"Right."

"Careful with this one. Everything by the book. We clear on this?"

"Yes."

"Okay, then, let's round up the troops."

As Reese followed Harris from his office, she could feel the electricity move with her to the squad room. The detectives looked like antsy schoolboys waiting for recess. She looked at Gus Miller, her partner since she'd been transferred here seven months ago. He, as usual, appeared calmer, leaning back in his chair instead of forward, always the contrarian.

"Listen up," Harris said, though he had no real need to call for their attention. It'd been a slow morning all around and so he spoke to a rapt audience. "We've got a call from the Ascot Towers. Woman says a girl got murdered. We don't know much else yet so put your kid gloves on. I don't want any screwups. I need three teams over there now."

As Harris made the assignments, Reese moved across the room, took her place beside Miller. Her partner was standing now, as were the four other detectives Harris had picked.

"Reese and Miller are on the wife," Harris said now. "Pick them up in the lobby, and do it quietly. Don't bring the hotel into it. You're looking for a man with a golf bag."

"At the Ascot?" Miller said. "How many we going to stop?"

Reese chewed her lip to keep from grinning.

But Harris, who ordinarily liked Miller's jokes, looked annoyed. He said, "You hear me say Towers, Miller?"

"Yes, sir."

"Then I think you'll figure it out. Now get out of here. All of you. Clock's ticking."

The detectives headed for the basement garage. As soon as Reese and Miller were in their car, Miller said, "So what've we really got?"

"Big fish. Don't know much else but the name: Santerre. You heard of him?"

"Yeah, one of the quiet rich."

"Huh?"

"You know. Birth, marriage, death type."

Reese started the car, began guiding them out to Forty-second Street. "No, I don't know," she said. Though she had more years on the force, Miller had spent a lot more time in this precinct—Midtown. The high-rent precinct, or, more accurately, the one where high-rent meets low-rent. Reese had done most of her time in the Ninth, where she liked to think things were more real. But then things down there had become a little too real.

"You know," Miller said again, "only times you should be seen in the paper. That kind of guy."

"Is he?"

"How should I know? That's the whole point with those ones. Never knowing."

It annoyed Reese that she still had to rely on Miller. But the idea of doing as he did—cross-referencing the business section with the society columns—annoyed her more. "So what else do you know?" she asked.

"Mogul of some sort. Privately held company, I think. Privately controlled anyway. Beyond that, you got me."

"So what's the big deal about the Towers?"

"Ultra, ultra. Small, discreet. Place those kind of people go when they don't want to be bothered by anyone, seen. Hey, what else do you know? What the hell got into Harris?"

"Looks like this one's being watched from on high, though how high I'm not sure yet. Said to play careful. Everything by the book."

"Oh, great."

"What?"

"Them throwing big fish into our little pond. That's never good. You know what I mean."

"Why don't you tell me."

"They either want 'em caught a certain way, or thrown back."

The hotel was close by, just a few blocks east and north. Reese parked out front. The other two cars pulled in behind her. She made the obligatory badge display to the desk clerk and then the six detectives took their posts.

The tight lobby would serve them well. An L-shaped desk led to the elevators—two on each side of a relatively narrow hall. One team moved to the far end of the hall, blocking a revolving door there.

The other team waited on the near side, where the desk began. Reese and Miller positioned themselves a little farther back, where steps led to a small waiting area. They began the wait, trying to look inconspicuous, though in a lobby this small the six of them were a crowd.

Upstairs in the suite, Gabriel Santerre emerged from the bathroom. He found his wife standing, but for the moment he ignored her. He crossed the room, carrying his shaving kit, putting it down on the bed. He smoothed creases from the bedspread. There was a stain from the girl. The oil had made it linger instead of simply drying.

He went to his suitcase, a small travel bag, and found another clean shirt. He hadn't thought he'd need so many but was now glad he'd packed four. After putting it on he went to retrieve his cuff links and watch. Ingrid still stood by the table, hovering.

"Go on and get yourself dressed," he said.

His voice put her in motion. She went into the bathroom, where she began to furiously scrub her face. This meant that once the smeared makeup was gone, her face itself appeared blotchy. Her cosmetics were there, near at hand. From habit she began applying things—foundation, blush, concealer.

She stopped at her eyes. Had to force herself through these motions. She had to work hard to see at all what she was doing. Still, she managed it.

Once she'd accomplished all this she had the sense of having done it wrong, or backwards, because what she wanted now, most of all, was a shower. She considered starting again. Got so far as to open the shower curtain, which her husband must've pulled closed. But then there it was— the same tub, impossible to even consider stepping into.

She closed the curtain quickly. Bathed as best she could in the sink. Did this in a rush because she wanted away from the tub. Out of the bathroom.

She gathered her things; returned to the bedroom still with a sense of hurry. Before she'd had the idea she should stall, give the police time to arrive. But now she just wanted out—of this room, this suite, this hotel. By now she believed calling the police had been simply another of her daydreams.

Santerre had adjourned to their sitting room. His valise was on the floor beside the golf bag. Her makeup case sat on the table near the phone. She put the cosmetics she was carrying inside it, tossing them on the little top shelf, then closing it. Next she put this case beside the other two, near the door. The little padlock on the burgundy bag stilled her urge to peek inside. Unaccountably she wanted a last look.

Instead she set about getting dressed. She had no change of clothes, not even clean lingerie. As usual, her husband had surprised her with this getaway, saying he'd packed for her, which meant only that he'd brought her makeup case.

She found her things—her clothes—neatly folded on a chair. He must've done this because she certainly hadn't. The last she'd noticed they were strewn across the floor.

She took her stockings and garters. Began with these, though they were intricate, seemed to slip from her fingers again and again. She sat in the chair finally. Had to do this to be able to put the stockings on. The camisole was easier, her blouse and skirt not difficult, though she'd had to get back on her feet.

Putting on her suit jacket let her almost feel ordinary, if only for a moment. Just as quickly the weight of pretending this sent her back into the chair. Her eyes focused on the golf case, then blurred. She thought she might cry except this was something she hadn't accomplished in years.

The sickness in her stomach, the discomfort that had signaled the need to weep, soon turned to a simpler nausea. It was a more familiar sensation, but one she never acted on either because invariably it came when her stomach was empty. And, too, usually it found her like this—immobilized.

The heaviness of the room held her down, being alone in it with the girl. Ingrid worked hard at pretending her away, at imagining golf clubs, and towels, and tees in that heavy case shaped not quite right.

Her husband's voice broke through this. It reminded her of the way she needed him. How much she depended on him in situations like these. Put away any understanding that he was the cause of these situations, replacing it with only the sense that he rescued her from herself.

He'd said, "You've dallied so long I've had to pay for another night."

She held onto these words. Pulled herself to her feet with them. Felt oriented now that things were again her fault.

Santerre had employed the express-checkout option. He'd extricated them by way of the television set and the remote control. He enjoyed the efficiency of this but he missed walking to the desk, handing his key to a clerk instead of leaving it in the room. As with wearing the belt, these were small pleasures. A less practical man, a weaker man, might've succumbed to the need for them.

He picked up the bags and Ingrid fell into step. She carried her makeup case, held the door for him. They walked down the hall to the elevator, rode alone to the lobby.

As soon as the doors opened, two men approached them. And then two others. Ingrid had to force her mind to keep still. She'd forgotten this—the existence of other people. And she couldn't discern what these men were saying. She stood there, oblivious of her connection to this event. She and her husband had again become a single entity, and so when one of the men suggested she step away, then insisted, she opposed him.

"Ma'am, please step aside."

She heard these words again and again without the ability to attach meaning or action. She felt a firm hand on her arm, and then a gentler one as a woman took her makeup case and escorted her through the cramped lobby. Ingrid turned back to see her husband surrounded by four men. One held the suitcase, another the golf case, a third and fourth had her husband. She saw the small glint of metal, the display of a badge. Had this been what she wanted? Really what she wanted?

Three   The crowded noise of the Manhattan sidewalk disoriented Ingrid all the more, and the crisp November air did nothing to clear her head. She relied on the steady grip of the policewoman to guide her through the Monday lunch-hour bustle, guide her to a waiting car. None of these police people wore uniforms, and the car, too, was plain, unremarkable.

The woman got into the backseat with her. She sat beside Ingrid silently. Her hand had released Ingrid's arm and, without thinking, Ingrid turned her head to the hotel doors, saw her husband coming out through the near one, the one to the right of the revolving door.

They'd handcuffed him. An unfamiliar overcoat hid this, but it was obvious nonetheless. Two men walked on either side of him. The other two followed behind carrying the luggage—one with the misshapen burgundy case, the other with her husband's travel bag.

She craned her neck, saw her husband put into a second car. The open trunk obscured the rest. Blocked her view so she couldn't see them hoisting the girl, dropping her in there. Even unseen this seemed terribly cruel to her.

And separating her from Gabriel. This too felt cruel and off-kilter. All of this did. Why had they listened to her? She struggled to remember the phone call. What she had said for them to have taken her so seriously. To have taken her at her word. A thing she hadn't experienced in so long that it now made her nauseous.

She turned her head again, sighting the metal grate, the back of a driver's neck. Her head pitched forward, lifeless. Her chin sank to her chest, her eyes closed. When the ignition key turned, the noise was deafening. The motion of the car pulling from the curb caused a small cry to escape her.

She felt the policewoman's hand again. Then an arm around her shoulders. She let herself rest against the woman, and in this moment she thought of Nina. She tried not to, believing she shouldn't bring Nina into this, not even in this way, in her mind. But she couldn't help herself.

They arrived at the station house. Ingrid climbed stairs and stairs with the woman at her side and the driver leading the way. She wondered if she'd ever be able to find her way out of here. Twists and turns confused her—the bumps and knocks of people passing by.

At last she found herself in the stillness of a room, sitting at a table, sipping tasteless coffee from a paper cup. The coffee, too, reminded her of Nina. The mornings they'd spent together. The comfort of them.

She tried to focus, to let her eyes fully open, to hear what these same two people were saying. But what she heard instead was her own voice saying insistently and anxiously, "Where have you taken my husband? What have you done with him?"

"Ma'am, ma'am."

That word she detested kept filtering through. She

couldn't acknowledge it, especially not when spoken by this strange and thick young man before her. The simple sight of his huge hands pressed flat against the table, his bulky forearms, had rendered her speechless. Then there was the woman's hand coming into Ingrid's field of vision, touching one of those forearms.

The man stepped away from the table. Ingrid's gaze didn't shift. She saw the woman's waist first, a thin belt cinched her pants. Ingrid measured it, deciphering what it could accomplish if employed in her husband's manner. But then it dipped below the edge of the table as the woman sat down.

"Mrs. Santerre," she said, "Mrs. Santerre, listen to me a minute. You placed the call."

Ingrid raised her eyes to meet this woman. She became briefly lost in the policewoman's hair—long, soft curls flowing a little past her shoulders. Her gaze followed them. She let her head dip and then come up again to find the woman's eyes, deep gentle eyes, brown. So like Nina's that Ingrid found her head dipping down again, and so when the woman said, "Yes, that's right," Ingrid realized she appeared to be nodding.

"No, no it isn't," she said quickly.

"You didn't make the call?" the policewoman said, clearly not believing, coaxing.

"You don't understand. You couldn't possibly understand."

"Ma'am, I think we've got a pretty good idea what's happened here."

This was the man again. His voice intruded, breaking the moment in halves, pulling Ingrid's eyes to him in a way that hurt, so she put them back to the woman and there it was again, the illusion that she was shaking her head.

"Gus, why don't you leave us alone a minute." The woman said this without looking at him. Her eyes stayed with Ingrid's, held her.

When Ingrid heard the door open and then close, she said, "Can you understand?"

"I'm trying to, Mrs. Santerre. I'm Detective Reese. We want to help you, but first you need to help us."

Gabriel Santerre had been taken to an adjacent room. He sat at a table surrounded by four detectives, the same four who'd brought him in. Glorified bellhop, he thought as one of them lifted the burgundy bag, plunked it before him on the table.

"You want to tell us what's inside," another of them said. This one stood directly across from Santerre. He was leaning, hands near but not touching the case, his torso on a slant, suspended above it, and his face so red and determined Santerre smiled.

"Am I being arrested?" he asked plainly.

"We'll get to that. For now just tell us what's inside."

"I'd like to call my attorney."

They, of course, attempted to convince him this wasn't necessary, or even desirable. They employed every insipid trick and argument in their armory. One after another they did, each taking a turn, to which Gabriel Santerre said absolutely nothing.

He wondered at their not just opening the case. To have brought him here, to have taken things this far—he didn't believe they couldn't open it. He kept himself abreast when it came to this type of law. Sitting, watching them, he began to believe this was not simply a strategy, another pathetic game on their part. No, he surmised they were squeamish.

Once he'd determined this he observed them in a different manner. He noticed how they avoided touching the case, recoiled if they did so accidentally. He marveled at this. He found himself invigorated by his contempt. And from this sensation emerged the desire to put them in their place.

Initially he stilled this. He did not give into it. He calculated parameters. Ascertained the exact distance he could go without losing his advantage. What he could do before the act of enjoying his desire would give them something they might want, something they could use—satisfy them.

He decided upon stroking the case, fondling it really. He did this with one lazy hand. His fingertips tickled across the vinyl. A gentle repetitive motion, and through it he was thinking, wishing, actually, that he'd purchased a leather case and not this piece of trash. But he forgave himself this. He couldn't have known he'd be in the position of touching more than the handle.

This brought his thoughts to his wife. That she'd accomplished this. That she'd put him in this position. It was another thing to marvel at. It gave him a sense of future, of promise even. An admiration for her, though this he would only reveal by the retribution he'd exact.

That same smile came again to his face. And he continued the stroking. Never for a moment did he let up and he never varied the motion. His actions had a curious effect on the policemen. All but one exited the room. Not together, but one after another. And so he believed he'd assessed things correctly.

Reese had remained with Ingrid. The detective still sat across from her, gently working. Ingrid now rested her arms on the table. She had her hands clasped together and Reese mimicked her movements. They leaned toward each other intently, intensely.

Reese said, "Why don't you tell me what happened."

Ingrid drew back, though there was no visible sign of this. Her body stayed the same, but maybe this woman had seen the change in her eyes because she let one hand touch Ingrid's hands. Stroked them in a way that loosened their grip.

The sensation left Ingrid giddy, dangerously so. This woman might loosen other things in her. Everything, the years of it, might pour out. Spill onto this table and how could this woman ever hope to mop it all up? No, she would drown in it.

Ingrid tried to shore herself again, but it was already much too late for this. Despite her efforts not to, she began talking.

"There was another girl," she said, meaning Nina. "Years ago." She paused, calculating in her head—the exact number mattered to her. About this she would be precise. "Seven years ago. You remind me of her."

"Mrs. Santerre, I need you to tell me about *this* girl. How *this* happened."

But Ingrid continued as if not having heard. She counted the years that had passed since Nina. "She'd be twenty-one now," she said at last, proud for having done the sum. "Much younger than you, of course, but . . ."

"Is she dead, too?" Reese asked bluntly.

"No," Ingrid said, drawing her hands away quickly, nearly getting to her feet before collapsing inside. She'd wondered this countless times. But not in the conventional way this detective meant. Her indulgence of herself, her failure; she'd no idea what it might've cost. And she'd begun telling this from that same place. Believing incorrectly, but nonetheless believing, that what she had to say might kill this woman who now sat before her.

But her own need had become too large to contain. It kept slipping and seeping. Her patchwork could no longer dam it. She'd been warring with it too long. Warring and losing since Nina. Nothing but feuds and floods, and blood, Nina's blood. So many nights and days awash in it because this she knew—he'd had her cut. He'd proved that much to her. Sent men to do it because he would not engage in something so base and untidy. And he still always wore that awful necklace—a constant reminder.

"Mrs. Santerre. Mrs. Santerre?"

It was Reese again. "Tell me your name," Ingrid said because it was all she wanted now. To know this woman's given name, to have this woman tell her her name, something Nina had never done. She'd learned by accident, or necessity really, that Nina was merely her working name, not the one she called herself. And stubbornly Ingrid clung to it, never using the real name, not even in dreams about her.

"Tell me your name," Ingrid said again.

"Mrs. Santerre, I'm Detective Reese."

"No, no, Sweetheart. I'm not so . . . Your given name." And with this request Ingrid met the detective's eyes.

"Mrs. Santerre," Reese said again.

The sound of her husband's name hurt too much. "Please stop saying that. I'm Ingrid. Please call me Ingrid."

"All right, then, Ingrid. You need to tell me what happened."

FOUR   In the other room Gabriel Santerre still tickled his fingers across the case. The one remaining policeman, detective, stood away from the table, his arms crossed tightly against his chest. He said nothing.

Santerre waited it out for a time, wanting to see if he could actually make this man squirm. He grew tired of this quickly, though. It provided no real challenge. He said, "I'd like to make that call now."

Santerre noted the way the detective looked at him, strangely it seemed. When he opened his mouth, he appeared to be going to say one thing but then, defeated apparently, he said another. "We'll arrange for that as soon as possible, Mr. Santerre." Having said this he made his exit, leaving Santerre alone.

By now, Reese had left Ingrid as well. She stood in the hallway with her partner and the other detectives. When this last one emerged from Santerre's room, he asked her, "Did you get anything from the wife?"

"Not much, except this doesn't seem new to her."

"She ask for a lawyer?"

"No."

"Well, he has. He's not giving a hint."

"You let him call?"

"Not yet, but there's no point stalling him. It's not going to make any difference."

"Give me more time with her," Reese said.

"You go back in if you want, but I'm giving the guy his call. You've got till the lawyer shows."

"Hold him up, okay? Talk to me before you let them together."

"Yeah, yeah, okay, but work fast. I don't think you've got long," he said, and then he went back to Santerre. The other detectives milled about. Reese edged closer to Miller, said quietly, "Keep an eye out, okay? Make sure I get told when that lawyer gets here."

"You got it," Miller said.

Reese went back to the room, back to Ingrid. "Mrs. Santerre," she said. "Ingrid, listen to me. Your husband's called his lawyer. I think you should do the same."

Ingrid smiled, "Tommy's coming?" she said.

"This isn't going well, Mrs. Santerre. You need to give me something, or you need to call someone."

"Why? Tommy will straighten everything out."

"Is there someone you can call? Do you have your own attorney?"

"Whatever for?"

"You're not on the same side."

"What? What is it you're saying?"

She said this as if hearing was the only difficulty, and so Reese responded in kind, raising her voice. "Mrs. Santerre, you're in serious trouble here."

The words hung between them, did so for an instant before disappearing into the gulf that was Ingrid. She sat there uncomprehending. Reese wanted either to shake her or embrace her. Wanted to do both because her sympathy for this woman was colored with anger—a purple fury, the color of the bruise now showing along Ingrid's jaw. Reese's eyes had gone there, so she tried that tack, said forcefully, "He did that to you, yes?"

Ingrid said nothing but Reese noticed a slight change in the woman's eyes as she moved her hand to her face. Seeing a way in, Reese said gently, "Does he hit you often?"

Ingrid's hand dropped to the table, thumped there, lifeless. "I'm clumsy," she said. "I'm a clumsy person." The words came from her sounding practiced and inert.

"Oh," Reese said, unable to resist sarcasm. "So, you bumped into something? Hit yourself?"

"That's right." The woman's eyes had turned fierce, carried the ferocity of a trapped animal, but her voice remained flat.

Reese changed tacks. "He's done this before, hasn't he, Mrs. Santerre? Killed some girl. Where were you on those occasions?"

"I didn't say that. Nina's alive. I told you she's alive."

"And she's the only other one?"

"I never said he did anything to anyone."

Reese pushed harder. "Where is this Nina person now?"

Ingrid didn't answer.

"Come on, now. Isn't she alive?"

"No. I mean, yes. She's alive."

"Then where is she?"

Still nothing.

"In some favorite landfill of his? Of yours?"

"No. You don't . . ."

Reese had wanted to go gently, but as that approach had yielded nothing she raised her voice another notch. "I don't what?" she asked harshly.

"Understand," Ingrid replied. A catch in her voice stumbled the word.

"Explain it to me then," Reese said, still playing rough, and hating it. Hating that she knew it would work.

"I tell you, I can't," Ingrid said, close to pleading now.

And the more the fissures and cracks began to surface, the more Reese had to fight to stay hard, to keep her objective in mind. She believed, perhaps incorrectly, that she could easily break this woman. That it was merely a question of yelling and screaming—of berating Ingrid until scattered bits of her littered the table.

Reese believed she simply didn't want to resort to this unless it was absolutely necessary. Unless she could be sure it was for the woman's own good. So Reese had retreated when she said, "Tell me what you can, then. Tell me where Nina is."

Hearing the name sent Ingrid rambling dreamily. Reese cursed herself for going soft. But she still couldn't recapture her cruelty. "Tell me where she is," she said, but with little effect. The woman before her kept babbling.

Reese would not make the same mistake again. She raised her hand, sent it slamming against the tabletop. She pushed aside the hint of satisfaction she felt as Ingrid cowered. "Where is she?" Reese demanded, yelling at the woman now. And, yes, it did work.

"In Westchester," Ingrid said. "Bedford. It's not far from our home."

Ingrid gave the address, and when Reese kept at her, the name—Carver, Lynn Carver.

"So you still see her," Reese continued, letting up just a little.

"No. I didn't say that."

"You don't see her?"

"She won't see me." But here Ingrid's eyes closed. Her head dipped forward.

Reese didn't want to lose her, couldn't be sure just how lost she'd become. The way the woman's head lolled made Reese fear for her. "Mrs. Santerre," she tried now. And, despite her earlier resolve, she asked softly, "Do you understand where you are? What's happened here? What's happening?"

"What?"

"Do you know where you are?"

Ingrid appeared ruffled, but brought back. Her tone was somewhat indignant when she said, "I can't say precisely, if you mean street address, that type of thing."

This curious response left Reese unsure if the woman was further gone than she'd thought or more present than she'd ever imagined. It left her suddenly unsure who was working who.

There was a knock on the door. Reese got up and cracked it. She nodded at what Miller told her. Things would happen quickly now.

Fiue "Tom," Gabriel Santerre said heartily, as if meeting someone on the first tee. He didn't get up, though. He merely extended his hand across the table, across the bag, which still lay there undisturbed.

"Mr. Santerre," Tom Burns said with somewhat less enthusiasm. He found a place on the table for his briefcase, then sat across from Santerre. "How do you want to do this?" he asked.

"That all depends," Santerre said as if the options were inexhaustible. "Where does it stand?"

"They won't open the bag."

A moment's displeasure crossed Santerre's face before he recalibrated, discerning that what he'd gained far outweighed what he'd lost.

Burns kept talking. "They're playing carefully. They don't want to make any mistakes. But they were counting on your wife."

Santerre snorted at this, then laughed. A low, crackly, chuckling sound.

"She dummied them," Burns continued. "Now they're in stasis. It's our move."

"Well then," Santerre said, "it seems she's made this easy for us. What happens to the bag?"

"Seized as evidence if a charge is made. Otherwise you walk out the door with it."

"Can they make a charge?"

"They won't let this go easily. But they know who you are. They knew before I arrived, which explains their caution."

"So the question is who they charge."

"That would seem to be the situation."

"If we hit her hard, how lightly can I go?"

"Underage?" Burns asked, nodding slightly toward the bag.

"Presumably, but how could I know this?"

"Speaking pessimistically, I'd say statutory plus accessory after the fact. Of course you're capable of cooperating extensively. Your wife, it would seem, is not. It appears we could make this easy on almost everyone, if that's your thinking."

"We give them the bag."

"It would make sense. Without it they have nothing, but they won't simply let this pass. They could still open it. They may just be waiting for a go-ahead. If you walk with it, they'll watch what you do with it. Surrendering it is likely the correct opening."

"Immunity."

"In exchange?"

"That's right."

"I'm uncertain whether that's possible."

"Well, then, you need to talk to someone."

"How much do you want to give up at this stage?"

"Nothing. Immunity in exchange for my cooperation. That's what you tell them."

Reese had kept at Ingrid, even more insistently. But now that Santerre's lawyer had arrived, she pursued a different course. "Do you have your own money?" she asked.

"My husband handles those things. He has me sign papers. There is some property in my name."

"What about a bank account?"

"No, I don't think so. He gives me money."

"You need a lawyer."

On this point Ingrid continued to balk. "I don't understand you. Tommy's always handled everything."

"Look, I know someone you can use." Reese crossed a line with this—offering a lawyer at all, let alone a close friend of hers. "I'm going to make the call for you." And with this she left the room.

Reese went to her desk and placed the call. She wondered how she'd ever entice her friend away from that downtown corporate firm where she now seemed so at home. Reese hadn't planned a strategy for this. She hadn't had time. She'd offered her friend's services impulsively, instinctively. Reese had gambled. And now her call funneled all too quickly from receptionist to private secretary. But there it stopped abruptly. A crisp voice told her Ms. Coffey was on another call, asked her to hold.

In those moments, Reese almost bailed. But then Eleanor Coffey's harried voice was on the line. "Caroline," she said. "What is it?"

"I need you. There's something going on up here. I need you for it."

"Okay, I'm on my way."

Reese put down the phone, surprised and relieved Eleanor hadn't put up a fight. She'd expected one, given her friend's fiery departure from the DA's office some months ago. Eleanor'd sworn off *the entire fucking system*, as she'd come to call it angrily and consistently. But before Reese had more time to wonder about her friend, the door to Santerre's room opened and Tom Burns emerged.

"Hey, anyone out here want to talk to me?" he called above the room's insistent noise.

Reese went to him quickly, before anyone else could. "What do you need?" she asked.

"You called a DA yet?"

"No," Reese said. "But it can be arranged."

She wanted to drag out even this small exchange, but Burns said, "You do that." And then he was swiftly back behind the door.

Miller stood at her side now. His wide palm on her forearm. "You get anything yet?" he asked.

"Not much. Just another girl. One who lived. That's where we go if she stays mute. You know what they're up to in there?"

"No, but I can guess."

"Yeah, me too. Look, I called a lawyer for her. I called Eleanor Coffey."

Reese waited a beat for his reaction.

He said only, "I'll let you know when she gets here."

"Gus, do you think . . . ," she started to say, before amending, before saying instead, "Will you get a DA for them?"

He nodded.

"Take your time, okay? Call that ADA, that tired one, Holmes. He ought to slow them down."

Miller smiled, "Yeah, takes him twenty minutes to open his briefcase. Hell, might take me twenty minutes to call him." He began moving toward his desk with exaggerated slowness. His joking helped her face those two closed doors again—his jokes and that he hadn't questioned her for calling a lawyer, for calling Eleanor. She knew he'd keep it to himself. That if asked he'd back her up, say Ingrid had made the request, and that Reese had simply recommended someone.

She still faced the two doors. She looked over at Harris's office, but she didn't see the lieutenant. The rest of the room bustled with the usual traffic. Normally all the hustle made her feel at home, but today she felt removed from it. She gave Gus one more look. He caught her gaze and she returned his smile. He picked up the phone as she turned to face the doors again.

She still hesitated, realized she wanted to enter the wrong room. That she wanted to know exactly what Santerre and Burns were planning in there. Instead she returned to Ingrid.

Six　　Eleanor Coffey arrived quickly. Before the DA. Reese met her in the hallway outside the squad room. They hadn't seen each other in a while and Reese found herself admiring Eleanor's hair. The short afro had more gray than Reese remembered, and noticing this, she realized she'd missed her friend.

"What've you got?" Eleanor said, already all business.

"A dead girl," Reese said, snapping herself back. "Picked up a couple trying to carry her out of the Ascot Towers in a golf bag. The wife seems shocky. Still not talking. Still covering for the husband. Looks like he's got a history of this. Looks like he's got a long arm, too. I've never seen so much tiptoeing around this place. We can't even get the bag open."

"It's Santerre."

"What? You know him? You know this already?"

"Word travels fast, particularly in my neck of the woods."

"What do you know about him?"

"Hard to know much more than the name," she said. "Very private man. Very powerful man. How'd you get them?"

"His wife phoned it in."

"Well, that's a start. The DA here yet?"

"Not yet. I told Gus to call Holmes, remember him?"

"That sad-sack ADA-for-life? How long you think I've been gone, anyway? Take me more than six months to forget that pencil pusher."

"Yeah, well, so I got Holmes. I figured he'd jam their circuits."

"For a while, anyway. Nothing going to stop a man like that for long. I assume his lawyer's here?"

Reese nodded.

"So, why am I here?"

"The wife. She's the only thing we've got on him, and she doesn't even get that her husband's lawyer doesn't work for her anymore. She's giving me next to nothing and, no doubt, they know it. Clear already how the husband's going to play. His lawyer's the one asked for the DA. She stays blind, deaf, and dumb, they'll cut a deal that cuts her to bits."

"Well, we'd better get moving. Let's have a look at her."

Once inside the interview room, Eleanor Coffey led off. She began simply enough: introduced herself, then added, "Detective Reese called me. I'm here to offer you counsel."

Ingrid barely stirred.

"Mrs. Santerre," Eleanor began again, but Reese interjected, saying, "Ingrid, this is the lawyer I told you about. It's time you started helping us."

Ingrid still didn't come to. Reese couldn't be sure if the woman had even registered Eleanor's arrival.

"Mrs. Santerre," Eleanor said again, her voice cajoling, as if she were speaking to a mischievous child.

There was still no reaction.

Eleanor tossed her briefcase on the table. The sound did

jar Ingrid. Her head snapped up, and when Eleanor took a seat, the scraping sound—chair against floor—made the woman wince.

Reese needed to decide where to put herself, whether to sit beside Eleanor or Ingrid. But instinct told her to sit between them. She picked up a chair, rather than pulling it. Put it down at the end of the table near the door. Once seated, she glanced back and forth between the two women.

Eleanor looked peeved and impatient; Ingrid, bruised and weary. Reese felt some mingling of the other two. An angry tiredness ignited and dimmed her all at once, threatened to overcome her.

There was a knock at the door. Reese answered it, finding Gus Miller there. He told her Holmes had arrived. Reese nodded and shut the door again, returned to her place at the table. "Holmes is here," she said to Eleanor. Then she turned to Ingrid. "Mrs. Santerre," she said, "right now, your husband and his lawyer are talking to a prosecutor. And you can bet they're talking about you. How to hang this on you. So how's about you start talking to us."

Eleanor injected, "Mrs. Santerre, it would be in your best interests to cooperate . . ."

Then Reese again, "Your husband's moving and moving fast. You don't do something and do it quick, no one here's going to be able to stop him."

Eleanor said, "You did want to stop him, right? No other reason you'd've called the police."

Reese said, "Make your bid now, or this game'll be over before you even know it."

Ingrid tried to distinguish between the two women as their voices overlapped, blurred together. And the things they said. Finally she put her hands over her ears. With this, the closer one, the detective, grabbed Ingrid's arm. Yanked it hard, sent it crashing to the table.

The move broke through something in Ingrid. She felt something shifting inside her before she recognized heat. She looked into the detective's eyes, for a brief moment she did, and then her head dropped again.

In the room next door Gabriel Santerre and Tom Burns sat together waiting. Their conversation had drifted from the matter at hand to other business. A knock at the door interrupted them.

Burns got up to usher in the prosecutor. He was a tall man, probably in his mid-forties, at least ten years younger than Burns and Santerre, than Ingrid. His clothes, well made but worn and out-of-date, gave away the dissatisfaction that years of civil service invariably cultivate. His slight slouch upon facing his adversaries only accentuated this.

Sizing him up, Burns shifted gears quickly. "Let's get this over with," he said dismissively. "My client needs to attend to other business."

"Your client tried to carry a body out of a hotel."

"Let's not begin at odds with one another. Mr. Santerre has offered his full cooperation. Without this you are left with conjecture. Nothing else."

"What do you want?" the prosecutor said in a nearly inaudible monotone.

Santerre saw the opening and took it. "Why don't you have a seat, Mister . . . ? Tom, did we even make our introductions?"

The prosecutor attempted to stand his ground, saying, "Oh, I know who you are, Mr. Santerre."

"Well, obviously, young man. But I don't know you. This leaves me at somewhat of a disadvantage, wouldn't you agree?" His sharp, sick-sweet tone made the opposite obvious.

"I'm Holmes."

"Well, Mr. Holmes, have a seat." Santerre indicated the chair opposite. Burns took his place at his client's side and so the two stared across the bag at Holmes. They watched as he obeyed, sliding his long frame into the chair and then pushing it back from the table. He kept his briefcase vertical on his lap as one might do on a bus or subway. He actually hugged it to his chest—a physical barrier between himself and the golf bag.

"Tom," Santerre said, "make room for Mr. Holmes to put his things down."

Burns leaned across the table to retrieve his briefcase. He, too, avoided direct contact with the bag.

Holmes set his briefcase down but left it closed. He said, "What is it you people want?"

Burns stepped in now, "Mr. Santerre will surrender the bag and offer his cooperation in exchange for immunity."

"What you're suggesting is impossible. We have the 911 tape. We know the wife made the call."

"Did she say that?" Burns asked, more curious than challenging.

"We know she made the call."

"Well then, what does that give you? What exactly is she supposed to have said? Did she implicate my client?"

"We all know what's in that bag."

"Really? Do we, now?" Burns said.

Santerre had grown impatient during this exchange. He leaned forward, placed both hands firmly on the bag. He jostled it as he spoke. "You're wasting my time, Mr. Holmes. If you can't make this decision, get someone down here who can."

Reese and Eleanor still worked Ingrid, but their rapid-fire tag-team barrages had yet to yield any result. Only when Reese made physical contact, pulling the woman's hands from her eyes or her ears, did they see any reaction at all.

Reese had just done this again—slammed the woman's hand to the table—when another knock startled all three of them. Again, Reese answered it. And again Miller was there, this time needing her.

She looked back at Ingrid, saw the woman's head dropping forward once more. Her chin sinking to her chest as if her neck muscles had been cut loose to allow this. The quickness of the motion, the slight rebound of the head before it rested—Reese felt a little nauseous. She looked away, looked to Eleanor, and said, "Keep at her." If Ingrid heard, she didn't acknowledge it.

Now, outside the interview room, back in the squad room, Reese was livid. Before Miller had a chance to say anything, she saw Holmes emerge from the other room. She'd always thought him the opposite of Eleanor—flimsy, ineffectual, but then that's why she'd picked him. Making his way into the hall he looked wrung out, more so than usual.

Reese moved to him, said, "What's going on in there?"

"They want immunity. I've got to make a phone call."

"You're going to give it to them?"

"I didn't say that, but if you people had just done your job, mine would be a lot easier."

"What's that supposed to mean?"

"He's sitting there in complete control. If you'd just opened the goddamned bag we wouldn't be stuck in this limbo."

"What were we supposed to do? Open it in some fucking chichi hotel lobby? That'd go over real well with the city. And if we'd done it here without a warrant? You'd be screaming at us for that. Telling us how we'd jeopardized your precious case."

Reese continued her rant but understood she was just stalling. That really she agreed with him. Knew this whole thing smelled bad. Like playing by the book in this instance meant playing by Santerre's book.

Holmes walked past her to the nearest phone. Miller stood nearby. "Where's the lieutenant?" she asked him.

"Called downtown."

"Already?"

"Before we even got back. That's what I came to tell you."

"Shit," she said, giving a nod to Santerre's room. "Who've we got in there anyway?"

He gave her a tense smile, said through pinched lips, "I guess we both know that."

"And I guess we're not getting that warrant."

"Not even for fucking Christmas," he said.

Reese looked at Holmes. He clenched the receiver, spoke heatedly, but before he'd even finished the call the squad-room doors swung open.

"My God," Reese said, "will you look at that."

But Miller was already looking. Harris walked in flanked by the chief of police and not just any DA, but Earl Cherney, who ran the whole city office.

Reese tried to catch her lieutenant's eye, but he merely noted her presence. The three men huddled a little longer before the chief turned and walked out. Soon after, Cherney went into the interview room, the nearer one that held Burns and Santerre.

Then the lieutenant's index finger pointed toward Reese and curled back. She and Miller moved to him. Reese started to speak, got as far as, "What, no attorney general . . . ?"

But Harris's voice stopped her here, and stopped her cold. "Get in that room," he said, pointing now at the nearer door.

Reese and Miller exchanged looks and then they obeyed.

Once inside, Reese took in as much information as she could. Santerre sat there, calmly, surrounded by men of various descriptions. There was Cherney, looking just like he did on television, the only other place Reese had ever seen him. He stood with Burns, had just handed him some papers. The two chatted amiably, both wore crisp blue suits, and Cherney looked so fresh. His easy manner made Reese look away. She looked at her fellow detectives—the ones who'd brought Santerre in—but she regarded them just as warily, had to look away from them, too. The only place she could rest her eyes was Miller, so the two of them traded uneasy glances.

Burns, having finished his conclave with Cherney, now behaved like a host or maître d', running the room, positioning people. He stood near Santerre, gesturing and talking in a way that made this seem like some social gathering. The detectives appeared taken in, were laughing at the things he said. Reese stiffened, let anger pump her.

She looked at Santerre again. The only one sitting, he still appeared taller, physically larger than the others. He *was* big, but not bulky. Santerre's size was refined, taking space with the assumption of ownership, without apology.

He was dressed meticulously, fashionably even. And his dark hair was combed straight back—something slick tamed the curl in it. But his eyes were the true trouble. Deep, brown eyes, like his wife's. Cold, but alluring, too. Open in a way that could draw you in while letting you know they could close off, close you out in an instant, and that this was something to avoid, something to fear.

Santerre had caught Reese looking at him. He smiled at her, acknowledged her presence, saying, "Ah, we have a lady among us."

Reese steeled herself against his gaze. She would not allow herself to be drawn in by him. She would not play this game in which her colleagues seemed already enmeshed and enthralled. She wanted a snappy retort. Something strong to say back to this man. But she understood the manipulation. She would say nothing, and she would not drop her eyes from his. So Santerre looked away first, but only because something else caught his attention.

It was Burns, now playing master of ceremonies. He still had those papers in hand. Reviewed them cursorily as if they were a program, then said, "Well, let's get on with it."

Reese felt sickened as the detectives jockeyed for position, each one trying to get a better view of the case. She faded back as they huddled closer. She wanted to watch not just the case, but how the others reacted to its contents.

There was a collective intake of breath as Santerre extracted a small key from his pocket, the kind that might lock a child's jewelry box or diary. He fit it into the little padlock on the golf case and turned it. Next he removed the lock, then removed the key from it, and placed the two objects side by side on the table.

He began to unzip the bag, but slowly, carefully holding it closed as he did. When he'd finished, he drew back the vinyl, not with the flourish she'd expected, but gingerly.

The sight inside? Instead of the horror she'd expected, Reese found herself fixated. Unable to evaluate the body, she stared into the girl's eyes. The head was at the end of the table nearest her, arched back. And Reese saw pleading in the eyes of this dead thing she could not yet recognize as dead.

Miller's low whistle intruded, not merely on Reese but on the room as a whole. The others stared at him as if he'd broken a rule of etiquette. And Reese stared at him, too, took in his morbid grin, tried to return it. He stood his ground and she stood with him, stayed connected because they seemed the only sanity in the room—the two of them, and the girl.

Reese forced her gaze back to the body. It was naked but strangely unblemished, except for ligature marks clearly visible on the neck. The arms drawn behind the back seemed held there, but by nothing. The thighs jutted out, ending in bended knees. Then there was nothing more to see—the calves and feet still hidden beneath burgundy vinyl. This finished it for Reese, convinced her this was not a living thing. That it would remain this way—not yet fully formed, wholly dead. Reese wouldn't be saving this girl.

And then, knowing he wouldn't be looking at her, Reese looked at Santerre. His expression was one of contentment. And he'd begun speaking. He'd begun weaving his tale. And when she wasn't expecting it, perhaps because she wasn't expecting it, he looked at her—Santerre did—as he said, "We all know how women can be."

"Oh? And how's that?" she said, the sound of her voice startling her because she hadn't meant to engage him.

"Jealous, my dear," he said, briefly meeting her eyes before wandering the rest of her.

Now, Reese wanted to tear into this self-satisfied man, berate her colluding colleagues—all of them, except Miller, were snickering, enjoying the joke on her. And, too, most of all, she wanted to break apart the already broken wife, shatter her complacency, her complicity. Break her so wide open she would have to see inside herself, see her hands in this. But as she could do none of these things, Reese contented herself with standing still, smoldering, taking it.

Seven   Ingrid still sat at the same table in the same room. The woman across from her—Coffey, she'd said her name was, Eleanor Coffey—had kept at her for some time.

When the other one had been there, Reese, Ingrid had felt something. Something disconcerting but at least familiar. This one left her cold, and, above all else, Ingrid sought warmth. She had sought warmth wherever she could find it. She'd become capable of almost anything to obtain it, or some semblance of it, though this was not something she allowed herself to dwell on. It was not something she let herself fully comprehend.

The other one had given her, well, not warmth exactly, but heat. Heat born of anger, but then that was what she usually settled for, the closest she could come. And without that heat, she and Coffey had arrived, finally, at silence.

At first Coffey seemed discomforted by this, tried to break through it, but then she'd grown resigned. At least that's how she seemed to Ingrid. Now it was Ingrid who couldn't bear the silence. She said without inflection, "Coffey," and let the name hang a moment before adding, "You must put up with a lot of teasing."

Ingrid watched the lawyer's face. She'd been caught off guard it seemed, looked nearly impressed. Ingrid couldn't know that years ago Eleanor Coffey had begun to evaluate people by how they responded to her name. Whether they ignored it or made uneasy jokes. The matter-of-fact approach Ingrid had taken ranked high on the lawyer's scale.

Knowing none of this, Ingrid simply felt something between them loosen. "Mrs. Santerre," Eleanor Coffey began, then said, "Ingrid, they're in there right now finding a way to hang you. You do realize this?"

Despite Reese's absence, perhaps because of it, Ingrid heard what Coffey said. The words gave no room for tangents. There was nothing to play with, and so she sounded weary and adult when she responded. "Did it not occur to you I might be guilty? Did it never occur to you?"

"Guilt is a large word. I'm speaking specifically. Do I think you killed that girl and put her into that bag? If that's your question? No, I don't believe that. Not for a moment. No one in this station house believes that. But as it's the easiest solution to a difficult problem, I expect they'll find a way to believe it. So you'd better give them something else to believe."

This was too plain for Ingrid, and so she began drifting.

Coffey still waited for a response, but getting none she pressed on, but in another direction. She said, "Tell me about the call. Why did you call?"

"I thought it would change things," Ingrid said.

"Change what?"

"Everything," she said, the word coming out in halves. Coming from her as two distinct words, and so she said, "Every single thing."

"So you wanted it to stop. You wanted to stop him."

"Oh, I expect it's too late for that. Haven't you already said so?"

They were interrupted. Reese came into the room without knocking, startling them both. Ingrid could feel Reese's presence but she didn't look at her. She kept her eyes linked with Coffey's. For a little while she did, but Coffey could not hold her. Ingrid felt her limbs go slack. Her head dipped forward. And when she raised it again she found herself looking at Reese as if against her will. And she believed she saw something different about her, in her.

Then the two were getting up, leaving her. A sound came from Ingrid unwittingly. It was Coffey who said, "It's all right. We won't be gone long."

In the hall, Reese and Eleanor Coffey reconnoitered. "So I've got her to admit calling, at least," Eleanor began.

"Yeah, well, we've got the tape for that. And he's got an answer for it. He's got answers for everything. And they're all in there hanging on every word. Except Gus."

"What's the man saying?"

Reese recounted Santerre's story as clearly and simply as possible. "He's saying she did it out of jealousy. That the whole thing was her idea to begin with. Picking up the girl. All of it. That this was her kink, not his. That she liked watching. First to have him watch, then watch him take over. That he indulged her. That this was his only failing, indulging his wife's whims, trying to keep her happy.

"He says she'd finished with the girl and left her for him. That she'd been the one to insist on tying her, though he admits he's the one who did it. Again to indulge her. He says he'd thought they were done. He'd gone into the bathroom and came out when he heard sounds. Found his wife strangling her. That he tried to stop her, but it was too late.

"That then he'd simply been protecting his wife. Covering up for her. He called it 'an understandable, habitual response.' But here's the kicker: He says that realizing how wrongheaded this was, he had her call the police. That he'd stalled so we would be there to pick them up. He's got it all worked out. It's like he's had this story ready for years. And they're all in there eating from his hand."

Eleanor leaned against the wall. "We've got to get her talking."

"Well, they're moving fast. He's already got the key to the door." Reese said this too harshly and felt annoyed for it. She shook herself, so much so it was visible.

"You okay?" Eleanor asked.

"Sure, fine," Reese said. "So what's your next move?"

"I can't stop what's already in motion. If he's walking, she's in the system. I should be able to keep her here for the night, maybe longer. Stall the arraignment. Not have her sent to Rikers or Bellevue. But unless we can find some money for her, that's going to come. And we can expect it fast. He's got so much pull we may not get bail, so even money may be moot. It's a toss-up where she goes. Hard to say which is worse. The way he's playing, it looks like he might prefer a nuthouse, so maybe we should angle the other way. I've got to think."

"No, you're right. I think he wants her quietly locked away. No fuss, no bother. He kept saying, 'My wife isn't well.'" This phrase had stuck in Reese's mind. She could hear him saying it now.

Eleanor said, "I've got to get on the phone. You go in there and baby-sit."

Reese hesitated, and again it was noticeable.

"You up to this?" Eleanor asked.

"Yeah, yeah sure," Reese said, but it was a bit longer before she moved, before she walked the very few feet to the door and felt the knob in her hand. And as she turned it she looked back at Eleanor, saw her already at a desk, picking up the nearest phone.

Reese sank into a chair across from Ingrid. Before she'd seen that girl's body, she'd thought she understood this woman. That beaten and battered was explanation enough. Not now. Now she couldn't explain her.

And she suddenly realized no one, herself included, had bothered to wonder who the dead girl was. Just another dead whore whose identity would be hard to determine, and, no doubt, meaningless. That's how they were all thinking by now. How Reese herself had been thinking until now.

So Reese asked the question no one had spent any time on at all. "What was her name?"

"I told you already," Ingrid said.

"No, *this one,* the one lying dead in there. What was her name?"

"They never use their real names. Surely you know this."

"Well, what name did she use?"

"I don't know. I don't listen to that anymore."

"Mrs. Santerre, that girl in there is dead. What was her name?"

"I told you, I don't know. Julie, maybe, or Jewel, something like that."

Reese continued, "Where did she come from?"

"How am I to know this?"

"You know, and you'll tell me."

"I tell you, I don't know."

"Really? Your husband says you do. Your husband says you ask for them."

"That isn't true."

"Oh, no? He's got a room full of detectives ready to believe him. But now you want me to believe you've no idea where he finds them? Well, I don't believe you. And I don't have time for this."

Reese got up, headed for the door.

"The hotels," Ingrid said. "Not the ones we stay in, of course, those other ones. The ones called hotels, but that are really . . . Well, I don't have to tell you what they are."

"Does your husband own one of those, have a business interest in one, anything like that?"

"I wouldn't know. He doesn't tell me his affairs."

"And you don't ask," Reese said.

There was yet another knock at the door. It was Miller again. He said, "They're finished. Time to take her downstairs."

Reese nodded to him but didn't move.

"You want me to do it?" he asked.

She nodded again. Then watched him gather Ingrid up, watched him half-carry her across the room, and then they were gone. She didn't stay long herself, just long enough to know they'd be out of sight by the time she went into the squad room.

Once in the larger room, she gravitated toward her chair, her desk, familiar things. She slipped into her chair, still sat there when the other door opened.

The whole lot of them emerged—first the small cluster

of detectives, then Santerre, Cherney, and Burns. These last three looked sated, as if they'd just finished an expensive meal, as if they should be holding brandy snifters and cigars.

Reese watched them pass, saw Santerre nod to her. She didn't acknowledge him. But the pull was there regardless, too strong to completely ignore. And in it, the temptation to just go along. The knowledge that in the short run it would be easier. Easier than trying to understand the truth of this, untangle it all, all the years of it.

Once they'd left, she got to her feet and went into their room. She wanted the sight of the girl to secure her resolve, to remind her why the truth mattered. But the body had been removed. In its absence, Reese sat in Santerre's chair. She was still there when Eleanor came in.

"Well, they'll keep her here for the time being," Eleanor said. "But I don't think we can hold off an evaluation for long. That's definitely the direction they're headed."

"Yeah, well, maybe she is nuts. Wouldn't you have to be to do what she did? So what's some head doctor going to make of it? Some shrink on their payroll?"

"That one we can short-circuit. They'll get their guy, we'll get ours. Someone sympathetic. And thorough, very thorough. It'll slow it down."

"Hell, I'm not sure I'm sympathetic. And him. He's so pleased with himself, so goddamned sure. Maybe the two of them deserve each other."

"Nobody deserves him."

"And who deserves her? Me? Still the girl. One of the first to make first-grade, but still the girl, and so I get to bring her in. Lucky me."

"I heard this one before."

"Yeah, yeah."

"And I know what you'll do. You'll do what you always do. You'll do what's right. That's why you made the rank, isn't it?"

But Reese said nothing to this. They both knew Reese's promotion and subsequent transfer to Midtown had come under the most difficult and murky of circumstances.

Eleanor quickly amended, saying, "Well, that's why you wanted to make the rank."

Reese said, "Yeah, well, maybe I'd like to keep it."

Eight   After Eleanor Coffey left, Reese stayed a little longer in Santerre's chair before returning to her desk. Once there, she looked at her lieutenant's office. Through the glass walls, she saw him calmly pushing paper. Needing to know where she stood, where he stood, she got up and crossed the room, knocked on his door.

Harris nodded to her, looking a little weary, looking like she was something he was expecting, but dreading—something he'd hoped to postpone.

Reese went in, but just stood there. She stayed standing until he finally had to say, "Sit down, Detective."

She did as he said, but still said nothing, just stared at him, gauged him.

"What's on your mind?" he asked, and when she still stayed silent he said, "Oh boy. If you're starting quiet it's going to be an earful."

She smiled in spite of herself. She'd liked Harris immediately. From their first meeting he'd felt familiar, comfortable, trustworthy even. Ever since, she'd had to continually remind herself she hadn't known him very long. That she didn't actually know him at all. She'd only worked here, under him, for seven months. And she invariably forgot that while she had good instincts, was always being credited for them on the job, certain people could still thoroughly deceive her.

People who called on things in her so old and patterned they disrupted her capacity for evaluation.

"Well," Harris said, "let me have it."

And so she began: "Are we just going to let this happen?"

"You'll have to be more specific."

"Come on, he's got the suits lined up, the papers in hand. No one's even bothered to ask what we got from the wife."

"So what've you got?"

"He's killed before."

"She said this?"

"No. Not exactly. Not yet, anyway. But she didn't do this. We all know she didn't do this."

"And how is it we know this? Women's intuition?"

She smiled again. Coming from him this was a spar, not a cross. "Come on, Lieutenant, what're we up against? At least let me know if I'm wasting my time."

"Depends how you're spending it."

She said nothing to this.

He leaned back in his chair, clasped his hands behind his head, then said, "Okay, here's the situation. I get a call from downtown, and, mind you, this is before I've even sent you all out. This is as soon as that man's name hits the switchboard, and once it does it hits every switch, lights every light. So while you all go over to the Ascot Towers, I go sit in a room with the brass. And I get told how it's going to play. And it's not some captain telling me. Not even the chief of detectives. It's the chief of this whole damn department. And Cherney? Well, he doesn't have much time for me because he's on the phone with the mayor. You getting my drift? You with me so far?"

Reese nodded.

"You heard of INISCO?"

"Drug company, right?"

"Not just drugs. Industrial chemicals, agricultural chemicals, all kinds of chemicals."

"And?"

"And Santerre *is* INISCO."

He paused here. Reese felt him waiting for her to latch on to what he'd just said. But she refused to relent, instead she stayed stubborn, coming back at him with "So?"

"So, Santerre's the kind of man who gets mayors elected. Mayors appoint police chiefs. Lieutenants work for police chiefs. Come on, Reese. I don't have to tell you how this works."

"No, but if you're telling me to lie down with it . . ."

"I'm telling you that I'm obliged to work within certain constraints. The immunity's done. He had that secured before he even asked for it. Nothing any of us can do about that. But you think the wife's innocent, prove it. You think Santerre's got something behind him, prove it. I'm not going to stop you. I might even give you a pretty wide berth." He paused again, waited for her to say something, but still she didn't. He leaned toward her now, said, "You think I like this?"

"No."

"But you thought maybe I did?"

"Something like that."

"Look, Reese, I'll let you and Miller work this as hard as you want. As far as you want. I'll even clear your desks. But you need to understand success and failure are likely the same thing this time. I may not be able to stop what happens to either one of you. Santerre's reach goes way beyond this city's limits. So you make sure Miller is apprised. Don't take him down unaware. And you keep me apprised. But don't tell your other buddies anything. Got it?"

"Yes."

"So where to?"

"Another girl. Lives out near Santerre's place. I want to run her and then go out there."

"Okay, I don't need more. Anything you need, you put through me. Directly through me. No shortcuts. Don't cut a single corner."

"Right."

She sat there a little longer. She stared at him until he said, "Well, go on then, Detective."

And with that, she left, went looking for Gus Miller.

She found her partner downstairs, still down in the basement. The processing was done, so seeing her, Miller said, "What's next?"

"We go after that girl."

"Huh?"

"The one I told you about. That one the wife kept talking about. The only thing she will talk about. I think that girl can fill the gaps. He's walking for this no matter what we do, so we have to find something else."

"Hold on a minute. You want to find some girl and then make a brand-new case from her? We don't even know what happened with this one."

"What? All of a sudden you're thinking like them?"

"No, that's not what I'm saying. I'm saying we need to

sort this thing out. Keep the wife from getting indicted maybe."

"You saw who was here."

"Yeah, okay, but at least find enough she doesn't go in a loser."

"That's what I'm saying. This is the way."

"Some girl?"

"Yeah, don't you see? We show he's done this before. Maybe a few times."

"And we base this on what? Some girl his lawyer will cut to pieces in minutes? Or better, they'll get it all excluded. Don't you think we should stick to this, to what's in front of us? Stuff's adding up bad. They found a belt in her makeup case, pieces of one, and the knife that cut it."

"Oh, and that means . . ."

"No, I'm just saying what it's going to look like, what they'll make it look like. He's thought this through."

"Obviously, but don't you see? We can use that."

Miller didn't answer. "You want some coffee?" he finally asked.

"No, I want to find this girl. Look, let's give it the rest of the day. If it doesn't go anywhere, fine, but we need some-one to back her up."

"So some girl, some hooker no doubt, that's going to make her credible? That's great, just great."

"Well, how do you want to do it? Sit around waiting for lab reports? Interview her again maybe? They'd probably manage to squeeze us in somewhere between all the shrinks lined up for her. Or, I know, we examine the crime scene. Talk to people at the hotel. Or how about we find out where he got the bag, like any of that matters now he's got those papers."

"Who're you turning me into?" Miller asked. "All I'm saying is they can get anything we find thrown out."

"So we don't try?"

"No, it's just . . . if we leave the details to . . . You saw how those guys were in there. You want them building this case?"

"No, but if we stick to this one . . . it's already decided. That's what they're counting on. Us sticking to this. They're three steps ahead of us. We've got to try a different tack."

"So now you're a mind reader?"

"No. It's just if we can find her. Find something they're not expecting."

"You've made your mind up."

"Just one afternoon."

"Do you even know where she is? She could be halfway across the country. Out of the country."

"No, she's right here. The wife gave her to me. Come on, give me a little room. Let's just run her name. See what comes up."

They did this, finding nothing but sealed suburban records. Nothing else. Nothing in the last seven years. It hadn't taken long to find nothing.

"Satisfied?" Miller said, throwing the printout across their desks.

"So, we go out there."

"You really think she's still there?"

"The wife says so."

Miller picked up the phone, said, "Well, let's see what the locals say."

"No," Reese said.

"No what?"

"You'll tip them off. If he's got this kind of reach here, imagine what he's got in his hometown. You want them to know we're digging around?"

He put down the receiver. "And your suggestion is?"

"We get in the car."

"I suppose you want to drive, too," Miller said, but at least he was smiling at her now.

Nine   The drive to Westchester, to Bedford, took less than an hour. The town itself was strangely unimpressive. They stopped for directions at a gas station. The attendant's instructions took them into a maze of dirt roads, interrupted at intervals with paved sections. The houses here were hard to see, set back, hidden by trees, or large hedges. Some behind walls.

They crawled around the roads, missing turns, retracing, literally going in circles until they found it—a smaller house. Out here you might call it a cottage. It, too, was set back from the road. Gravel from the driveway crunched under their tires, announced their arrival a little too loudly for Reese.

She hadn't pictured this. She'd expected an apartment building. That its anonymous doors and halls would give them an element of surprise.

"Think she's even home?" Miller asked, his voice hushed. The roads, the whole town had had this effect on them. They'd been talking in whispers for some time now. Even as they'd missed turns and house numbers, their curses came under their breath. So Reese whispered back, "Well, there's a car."

And so there was. Expensive, but understated, right there in the driveway in front of a garage.

"What is that?" Miller asked, Reese being the one who knew cars.

"I can't remember the name. French. Haven't seen one of those in a while."

They parked their boxy American car beside it. Got out slowly, carefully. Everything so still and quiet, disquieting. Reese felt like an intruder. She looked from the cars to Miller to the cottage, realizing you'd call it that only because of the wood and stone it was made of, not its size.

As they walked to the door she said, "Citroën."

"What?"

"The car, I just remembered."

"Oh."

Miller was the one who rang the bell. They heard nothing in response. Reese rang it again, leaned on it, but still nothing. She stayed put while Miller strayed a bit, drifted farther left, trying to peek in a window. Reese began knocking.

At last there were footsteps, not scurrying, but slow and deliberate. Miller ducked back from the window.

"Well, something's coming," he said, laughing too loudly, nervously.

Reese nodded slightly, barely an acknowledgment. Then a voice came through the heavy wooden door. Clearly a woman's voice but deep, saying simply, "Who is it?"

Reese said, "Ms. Carver?"

"Who's there?"

The voice was not what Reese had expected. Frailty, she realized now, was what she'd expected. She pressed on, "Ms. Carver, Detectives Reese and Miller, NYPD."

"What do you want here?"

The voice had notched down further.

"Ms. Carver, just open the door and we'll discuss it."

"You got a warrant?"

"No, no, it's nothing like that. We just need some information." Reese paused, deciding whether to play a card or whether it would make matters worse.

Carver said, "Well, I don't have any of that. Why don't you just . . ."

Reese cut her off, "Ms. Carver, do you know an Ingrid Santerre?"

There was nothing for a moment, long enough that Reese believed she'd miscalculated. But then the door opened. Standing before them was a tall woman, again not what Reese had expected. She'd expected a child, a teenager, not this imposing figure. She had to remind herself of Carver's age. That the woman before her couldn't be more than twenty—was still a girl, not a woman, somewhere between the two. And as she did this, Reese realized she'd thought Carver would look very like the girl who'd lain on that table encased in that bag. Instead Carver was intimidating. Impassive. But, nonetheless, the door was open.

"May we come in?"

"Suit yourself," Carver said, standing aside, letting them pass.

Reese stepped inside with Gus following. Carver led them to a sitting room, furnished simply but, again, expensively. The woman herself was dressed that way—simply, worn jeans and a shirt, but an expensive shirt, a man's shirt. And the shoes caught Reese's attention—loafers in a dark brown, Italian probably. They looked soft and comfortable like the couch Carver ushered them to. They sat down. Carver took a nearby chair and waited.

Reese met the woman's eyes, dark eyes, like Santerre's, like Ingrid's. Her hair, too, reminded Reese of Ingrid. That they should resemble each other was not entirely surprising. It made a certain kind of sense to Reese.

Carver interrupted her deliberation. Her voice impatient when she said, "Well?"

Reese stayed slow to disrupt the woman's pace. She said, "We need your help, Ms. Carver. Mrs. Santerre does."

"So? I'm listening."

"She's being held on murder charges, but we don't believe she's responsible. Her husband . . . You know her husband?"

"I knew him."

"We believe he's the one responsible."

"And what has any of this to do with me?"

"We think you can be of help to us."

"How's that?"

"You know her."

"I knew her."

"Then you haven't seen her since . . ."

"Since what?"

"She told me some things about you, Ms. Carver. She talks about you quite a lot."

"Does she?" Her voice quavered slightly. Her first seam.

Reese proceeded carefully, "Yes, she speaks of you."

"Saying what?" Carver's voice had turned hard again. She'd recouped already.

Reese stayed steady. She had no real answer for this so she evaded. "Reminiscences, I guess is what you'd call it."

At this Carver became sarcastic, but lightly so. "Ah, what a pretty word to attach to so much ugliness. Hers or yours?"

"Mine, I suppose," Reese said. "But if you don't like it, why don't you tell me how it really was."

Miller took his cue. He stood now, leaning on the arm of Carver's chair, was right up in her face, yelling, "Come on, girl. Stop wasting our time and get on with it."

Carver stared past him to Reese. "You want that?" she asked Reese.

Reese nodded.

"Then you get him the hell out of my house."

Without letting her eyes leave Carver's, Reese waved Gus away. He went, but reluctantly.

The two women waited for the door, waited until it had opened and then for it to close. Once it had, Reese said gently, "So, he's gone now. You can tell me, Nina." She used the name calculatedly, curious what the effect would be.

Carver got to her feet. She said, "You think I'm simpleminded?"

"Not at all."

"You think you can pull some little trick and make me woozy, jog my memory? Is that the idea? Well, it won't work. I can tell you that right now."

Reese waited her out, let her go on berating and insisting until she seemed to tire. Carver quit pacing about and when she sat down again it was beside Reese, on the couch.

Reese waited a little longer before saying, "It's only that she calls you that. She still calls you that. She won't use your real name and so I've come to think of you as Nina. That's all. No trick," she lied.

"What is it you want?" Carver asked in a voice that helped Reese remember how young this woman still was.

"I want you to tell me what they did to you."

Carver got up. She said, "I'll show you what they did." She untucked her shirt, then unbuttoned it, just a few buttons at the bottom. Done with this, she unfastened the top few buttons of her jeans.

Reese stayed very still. A broad scar faced her, as if the flesh had been sheared away all in one swath. It ran off center, from beneath the girl's stomach, down. Then disappeared where her pants, though unbuttoned, obscured it. A professional's work, though certainly not a doctor's. Reese was so stunned she nearly touched it. Instead she said, "They did this to you?"

"In their way."

"She did this?"

"He had it done. It's not the sort of thing he would engage in directly."

"And what about her?"

"She didn't . . . well she never does, does she? I expect that's why you're here."

"Never does what?"

"Interferes with his plans."

Reese had kept her eyes on the scar, but these last words of Carver's—the toughness in them breaking up, giving way— made Reese look into the girl's eyes. She saw only sadness.

Carver turned away. She tucked her shirt and buttoned her jeans. She seemed shy now, or modest, possibly even embarrassed.

She spoke with her back still to Reese. Began by saying, "I expect you know how I make . . . made my living."

"I surmised."

"Well, then you can see how something like this might interfere. Clever, don't you think? Very clever."

"No," Reese said, "I think the word you used before fits it better."

At this, Carver turned. Facing Reese, she said, "What word?"

"Ugly."

Reese watched Carver's face change. Watched it go from soft to hard. She waited for what Carver would say next and how she would say it.

"Well, that's my job, right?" The words coming ragged first, then turning crisp when she added, "I'm quite good at my job."

"Is that still how you pay for all this?" Reese asked. She made the question seem idle, neutral.

Carver didn't answer. She seemed to have tired again, but remained standing when she said, "Shall I show you out, or can you find your own way?"

But Reese stayed put. Had one last thing to obtain. She said, "You didn't seem surprised."

"What?"

"When I told you Mrs. Santerre had been arrested for murder. You didn't seem at all surprised."

"Not very much has the capacity to surprise me anymore, especially where that woman is concerned."

"But you don't think she did it. You said as much."

"Did I?"

"Has he done this before?"

"Shouldn't you ask her that? Or him?"

"Nina, I'm asking you."

Again using this name got a result, but a different one this time. Carver's voice trembled when she said, "I've shown you what he's capable of."

"But, Nina, has he done this before? That you know of?"

The repetition of the name made another chink in Carver. She worked to steady her voice as she said, "I only know of one, and only what she told me. Don't you people call that hearsay?"

"But there could be others?"

"As I said, nothing much surprises me."

"And the one you know about?"

"Ask her." And with this, Carver closed off. Did so, so completely Reese knew there was nothing to be gained by pressing her further, not now in any case.

As she got up, she said, "You've been of great help, Ms. Carver."

"Have I?" The woman said genuinely, and then she escorted Reese to the door.

Ten   Reese left the house to find Gus Miller leaning against their car. He looked bored, had resorted to tracing paths in the gravel with his toe. Seeing her, he perked up. Gave her a wave. "Get a load of this," he said, heading for Carver's car.

Reese joined him.

"Plain sight," he said, pointing at the floor mat.

A syringe poked from underneath.

"Probable cause," he added.

"Out of our jurisdiction," she said, watching him deflate.

"We could still use it. Scare her a little."

"It'd take a lot more than that to scare this one." She handed him the keys, said, "Come on, get us out of here."

Once they were back in the car, back on the dirt roads, Miller said, "So?"

"Huh?" Reese asked, lost in thought.

"What'd you get?"

"She said there was another one. That the wife told her about another one."

"Who?"

"I don't know yet. Look, there's something I haven't told you. Something you need to know."

"I'm listening."

"The lieutenant says we could end up bad from this. I should've told you before we came out here."

"Like I don't know this already? Can't see how it's lining up?"

"Can you see yourself out on your ass? Pension gone? Working security at some shopping mall?"

"Happens to the best of us. And the worst, I suppose."

"So, you're with me? Really with me? No matter how low this takes us?"

"Yeah, I'm in."

"You're sure?"

"Yes, I'm sure."

They stayed silent until they'd found the highway again. Reese spoke then, saying, "We need someone watching her. We need a team on her. And phone records."

"Why, what else did you get?"

"He had her cut up pretty bad."

"So, you worried about her, or suspicious of her?"

"Both. I sure don't want the one who's lived this long dead on my watch. And she's not going to cooperate quick and easy. We need something on her."

"So, this is my job?"

"Yeah, but it goes through the lieutenant. Everything does from here on in. We tell no one else what we're up to."

Miller gave that low whistle of his. It reminded Reese of the body. She tried to shake the image from her head, but where her partner took her was almost worse.

He said, "You think the lieutenant's okay?"

"We've got to hope so."

"Yeah, but maybe we shouldn't be counting on it."

They went silent again. As they hit the West Side Highway, Miller said, "You know we could put private security on her."

Reese said, "Whatever made you think of that? Planning your future already?"

"Seriously," he said. "There's plenty of guys moonlighting. We could probably even find someone who knows his way around out there, without being known."

"You think?"

"Well, I can find out anyway."

"Find out fast. If she's going to move, it's going to be fast. And I want to know who she gets on the phone to."

"So, I'll get someone."

"Tonight?"

"Yeah, okay, tonight."

"And you'll clear it with the lieutenant?"

"Yes, Boss."

"Oh, and we should check out the hotel houses. That's where he got the girl. I'm betting he's up to his elbows in one of those. The dead one's Julie, or Jewel, the wife said. We should see what we can get from that."

"Hey, I'm just one guy."

"Well, tomorrow, anyway. Hey, turn here."

"Huh?"

"Take Ninety-sixth, okay? Across to Fifth Avenue. I need to check in with Eleanor. See what's happening. Can you just drop me off?"

"Yeah, but isn't it way the hell downtown?"

"I need to go to her apartment. It's too late for the office."

"Getting late all around," he said.

Miller dropped Reese at Eleanor Coffey's building. She hadn't been up here in quite some time. When Eleanor had worked in the DA's office, Reese had been up here constantly. Now it felt odd to be back again, so she waited on the sidewalk a little while before going in.

The doorman still remembered her. He waved her by without calling up to the apartment. In the elevator, she fingered her keys, picked Eleanor's out from the others. The two had spent so much time together back then, working late, either up here or at Reese's, they'd finally exchanged keys. Reese missed all that.

Tonight, as the elevator doors opened onto Eleanor's foyer and Reese faced that lone door, she wished the doorman had announced her. She stood before that door for a few awkward moments, and then rang the bell.

She was relieved to hear footsteps, and then Eleanor's voice, saying, "Coming."

"Caroline?" she said as she opened the door.

"Is it bad timing?"

"No, not really. You surprised me."

"I just wanted to check in. See if anything happened."

"Yeah, where were you two, anyway? I couldn't get either one of you, and no one seemed to know where you'd gone off to. They said you weren't answering the radio. Don't cops have rules about that sort of thing?"

"The lieutenant's got us working back alleys."

"This was his idea, I suppose?"

Reese still stood in the foyer. To evade, she said, "Can I come in, or am I supposed to stand out here all night?"

"Suit yourself. You always do."

"And you want to offer me a drink maybe?"

"All right. And then you'll tell me what you've been up to?"

"Sure," Reese said, making her way to the couch. She plopped herself down and waited. Glanced around for changes in the room while listening to the familiar sounds of Eleanor fixing drinks.

Then Eleanor brought two heavy tumblers, handing one to Reese as she sat beside her. Reese took a large swallow, then put the glass down. She said, "We went to see the girl."

"The body?"

"No, Nina. Remember? The one she kept mentioning?"

"Vaguely. How'd you find her?"

"The wife gave her up. Before you got there."

"So what's your angle?"

"Get something else on him. You know, since this one's over. Didn't I tell you all this?"

"No."

"Well, it makes sense, doesn't it?" Reese said, trying to contain her impatience. She was tired of relaying information. She wanted someone to know by osmosis. Wanted Eleanor to, at least. "Doesn't it?" she repeated.

"Depends what you've got, or who you've got."

"This Nina, or Carver's her real name, she says the wife told her about another murder. Would've been years ago."

"And?"

"That's all I've got so far. That, and Santerre cut her up, had her cut up. She showed me the scar. Nastiest one I ever saw."

"That doesn't prove who did it."

"I know that, but I believe her."

"Yeah, but is anyone else going to?"

"Maybe not by herself, but the two of them together. Her and the wife. One plus one equals one. You think?"

"Maybe. If you can get something solid underneath."

"There's something dirty out there. We ran Carver, and the records were sealed."

"Well, if she was a juvenile. That's not unusual. Hell, it's standard."

"Will you stop playing lawyer for a minute and tell me what you think."

"No, what do you think?"

"I think it's the only way to nail him."

"And her? The wife, I mean?"

"Get her off in the process." Reese picked up her drink again. "Where is she anyway?"

"Right where you left her. I told you I postponed her island vacation. But I don't know if I've got another day left of that kind of thing."

"And Santerre?"

"Lounging at home for all I know. I couldn't get anything out of your people. I don't know if they're keeping an eye on him or not."

"And the evaluations?"

"Delayed. But not by me. They probably figure the longer she's caged, the crazier she'll appear. But I'm guessing here."

"Did you see her again?"

"No. I do have other cases."

"I'm just asking. Anyway, I ought to be going."

"Look, I'm in court tomorrow, so . . ."

Reese cut her off. "One of your newest neediest? PepsiCo? Or is it some private fortune this time?"

"I'm not going to defend my decision again," Eleanor said, but she began to anyway, adding, "Was I enriching the greater good in the PD's office? Or with my stint as a prosecutor? I'm not going to apologize for leaving the system you enjoy so much."

"No, why should you? Not when you can return to the lap of luxury. Go back to your roots."

This was a low blow and they both knew it. Eleanor, always having felt out of place. Not black enough, certainly not white. She came from a background just as privileged, but it hadn't gained her entry. She didn't have access to those environs. The ones reserved for those others she could never join. Not by means of her Ivy degree, her law-school rank. None of it had opened those doors. So she'd joined the fringes, only to find she didn't fit there either, and that not fitting there hurt more.

"I'm sorry," Reese said, and she was. She hadn't meant to open this old wound.

Eleanor did not truly accept the apology. She brushed it aside, saying, "So where will you be tomorrow?"

"Back out in suburbia, I imagine."

"I'll keep the brakes on this as best I can, but you better get something more for me, and fast."

Reese put down the drink and got up. She nodded to Eleanor on her way to the door.

"Caroline," Eleanor called after her.

"Yeah, yeah. I'll get you something real," she said over her shoulder. And then she was leaving, had left.

Eleven   Ingrid had spent these hours staggering between disbelief and a too-stark clarity. Her physical self, her
actual body, stayed static. It was her mind that swung back
and forth. She'd been in motion for short periods. Had been
allowed a shower, a change of clothes. They'd exchanged her
suit for ill-fitting prison garb, and thin canvas scuffs.

The change of clothes had tipped her over. Ever since
she'd continued listing. But she found it harder and harder
to retreat to the comfort of her dreams. She'd attempted
sleep, but it had come to her in fits and starts, remained too
shallow to provide her with rest or diversion. And so now she
curled in the corner of her bed, such as it was. Used the
blanket for a shawl in order to keep from touching the walls.

The large questions did not preoccupy her. Words like
freedom were quite meaningless. But, of course, she didn't
know much of freedom, never having had the opportunity to
acquire a taste for it. Control eluded her, too—the notion
that she completely lacked it. And though she'd become
used to exercising some measure of it, she'd also lived long
periods without any at all.

What preoccupied her then were small things, inciden-
tals, because her life to date, while difficult, had not prepared her for squalor, or for such a small enclosure.

She disliked wearing clothes she knew others had worn.

She disliked being without her things, using a common shower, washing her hair with the same peculiar-smelling soap she used to wash her body and her face. She disliked having this soap doled to her in increments by a matron who bore her designation too well.

And she disliked returning to this cell with still-wet hair. And that now, though the whole afternoon had passed and then some, her hair still felt damp. Because of this, it seemed, she could not get warm. So she huddled and shivered at times, hardly noticing these involuntary movements of hers. And for all her years spent in dreaming, this was something she'd never imagined. Enduring it for even these few hours was still quite unimaginable, and yet she was— enduring it. Enduring it in the small gasps that now passed for legitimate breathing.

No one had been to see her. And who she'd expected had changed as the hours passed, as the likelihood of anyone appearing became more remote. Initially she'd expected her husband. Tommy at the very least.

When the afternoon came and went without them, she began wishing instead of expecting. And her wishes surprised her. That detective crossed her mind too frequently, and the lawyer woman, too, though less often.

Now as evening seemed to have come and gone as well, she gave up even these wishes. She curled there in the corner, half-aware, and waited.

Outside Eleanor's building, Reese caught a cab. She gave the station-house address, though she wanted to just go home. She almost redirected the driver, but stopped herself. She knew she wouldn't sleep, not until she had more information.

During the ride she cursed herself for what she'd said to Eleanor. Reese had brought her into this because she needed her. Needed someone outside the system, but who knew it inside out, and from both sides. Eleanor was doing her a favor, a big one. And Reese was too busy picking old fights to even consider what walking those corridors again would mean for Eleanor.

Reese had liked things better back then. They'd become friends when Eleanor was still a PD. But when she'd joined the DA's office they'd become quite a team. In Eleanor, Reese had found the right person in the right job—someone who could help her make things happen, and happen just the way she wanted. A dream scenario for a detective. And so she didn't see—wouldn't see—that for Eleanor it was a nightmare. That she was being eaten away, until finally she became eaten up and fed up all at once.

And then Eleanor'd said she was leaving. That she'd decided to go corporate. This news hitting Reese just a month after her promotion, her transfer. She couldn't accept it, especially not then. Not so soon after her own nightmare— that whole mess Eleanor had helped pull her through. The fights then had been nasty. Reese had accused Eleanor of selling out. And when that wasn't enough she'd tried everything she knew, used everything she knew to keep Eleanor put, keep her where she wanted her. And, like tonight, she'd sunk so low as to hit her friend's sorest spot. Had been unable since to keep from hitting it, though she certainly derived no pleasure from it.

Reese knew she'd called Eleanor for more than just help

with this case. Though it was this case that had made her call, something about this case. There'd been plenty of other cases she'd wanted to call Eleanor for, but she'd stopped herself. This time she'd barely hesitated. As soon as she'd sat across from Ingrid, she'd sensed the undertow again. She'd felt its pulling and felt herself pushing back against it. And she knew this dragging sensation all too well. And she knew it caused her need for Eleanor.

And Reese knew, too, that this need provoked her anger. Because Eleanor would help her go under. She needed Eleanor to push her toward the current, into it and then under it, which she'd reluctantly learned was the only way through it, to be rid of it, if only temporarily. She needed Eleanor now as she had then, during that whole ugly mess, to keep her from drowning.

The cab pulled up at the station house, shaking Reese from these thoughts. She was slow to pay, slow to get out. But once inside, she went directly downstairs, walking briskly past the desk, the holding cells, rounding the corner to the alleyway. That's how she always thought of it, an alley.

She slowed a bit as she walked this narrow corridor with a guard in tow. The ceiling and walls were painted yellow, a dingy shade even before age and dirt had shabbied it. The light came from glaring bulbs housed in cages. The cells themselves had no light, dark little rectangles you stepped down into.

She found Ingrid quickly. She was the only one standing. Her arms dangled at her sides. Her face was as close to the bars as it could be without actually touching them. And she shifted her feet, standing on one and then the other as if she didn't want to touch the floor either. With a similar on-off pattern she struggled to get her breath.

She didn't seem to notice Reese, or anything else about her surroundings. Reese was right on top of her before she saw any change in the woman's expression.

Ingrid said, "Didn't you leave?"

"I need to ask you something."

"Oh, I see. More questions." Ingrid turned her head, ever so slightly, away.

Reese pressed on. "I've been to see Nina."

With this, Ingrid faced her. She said only, "And?"

"She's quite unusual."

"Yes, that's a way of saying it."

"I think she wants to help you."

Ingrid retreated into the cell. As she did, she said, "I doubt that very much."

"No, I think she will."

"So, she's taken you in? Or you're taken with her?"

"Ingrid," Reese said while motioning to the guard, having her unlock the cell. Stepping down inside it, Reese compensated for the physical closeness by using the husband's name. "Mrs. Santerre," she said, "tell me about Nina, and your husband. What happened there?"

Ingrid stood a few feet from Reese. From a fog, she began speaking. "He brought her one fall. She tried to be like the others, but she wasn't."

"Others?"

"Yes, well, she wasn't the first but she was the last. For me, she was. Even for him, for quite a long time. And the ones after couldn't compare. You see, don't you? Having seen her . . . how they could never compare?"

"Yes, but tell me what you mean."

"For us. Don't you see? For Gabriel, for me? Surely, you understand."

But Reese was slow to respond, didn't know how to respond.

A sliver of panic pierced Ingrid, gave her voice a piercing quality when she said, "You have to understand." But she startled herself with her own pitch. "You have to understand," she said again, forcing her voice back down. "She was like a daughter to me. We were going to run away . . . but I betrayed her."

Here Ingrid stopped, as if there was nothing more to say about it.

Reese said, "How?"

Ingrid looked confused. "What?" she asked.

"How did you betray her?"

"Me?" Ingrid said. "Me," she said again, this time emphatically, then, "She betrayed me."

"How?" Reese asked again, shifting with her. "How did she betray you?"

"She wouldn't leave. She loved him. She didn't see. My daughter was a stubborn girl. Obstinate, really. And she loved her father, but I suppose that's always the case. Isn't it always? They never love their mothers. I tried to protect her but she wouldn't let me. She hated me for it. She blames me for it, you know. She blames me for him."

"Your daughter does?"

"Yes, well, she should, shouldn't she?"

"And Nina blames you?"

"Nina? Nina's all right. Don't you see? She's all right. She can take care of herself. She made that plain, didn't she? She didn't need me."

Ingrid began walking the confines of the cell. Agitated,

furiously pacing, she came across the walls as if she wanted them to move from her path through force of will.

"Ingrid, sit down," Reese said, trying to ground her.

Reese watched the woman turn her way, regard her with a fierceness that then went slack. And as Ingrid's face collapsed, the rest of her followed. The woman had begun to sob and Reese let her stay where she was—standing, backed in a corner.

Ingrid was mumbling now, too. She said disjointed things Reese couldn't decipher. Little snatches of things, "I'm so sorry . . . ," and, "I didn't mean for it . . . ," things of this sort. Then Ingrid pulled back, slammed herself into the corner, and then turned into it.

Reese stepped back a few paces. She watched the woman, noted mechanically the number of times Ingrid raised her fist and let it pound the cinder block. Each time it thumped the wall with a muffled thud. These blows assumed a rhythm and soon Reese lost count, wondered why she'd been counting to begin with. She let Ingrid wear herself out. Finally the woman staggered back to her bed.

At this moment the detective began again. She said, "Tell me about Nina."

Ingrid said calmly, "It was such a long time ago. I don't think about it."

"But you do think about it. About her."

"Do I?" Ingrid said, losing herself in Reese's voice, the echo made by the too-close walls. The words Reese had spoken echoed, too, reminded Ingrid of things Nina had said, similar things ringing in her ears, and then ringing 'round her. And so she felt captive again, by the way her life went around in circles and now finally circled her.

"I don't know how I've got here," she said aloud.

"I'm trying to get you out of this," Reese said. "You need to tell me about it."

"Didn't she?"

"Not very much. She said there was another one. She said I should ask you."

Ingrid crouched into the corner.

Reese said, "Ingrid, Ingrid listen to me. You've got to do this. We've got to do this."

"I can't," she said.

"Look at me," Reese said, but Ingrid kept her chin tucked. She closed her eyes because they hurt, aching dry from tears she couldn't cry. And her throat becoming this way, too, scratchy, achy; closing off.

She felt Reese's impatience, grew scared of her leaving but still she would not open her eyes.

"Look at me," Reese said again, this time harshly.

Ingrid opened her eyes. She saw the detective still standing, looming, her hands outstretched. Ingrid looked for her own hands. Then found herself getting up quickly, pummeling at Reese, ineffectually, unaccountably.

Reese simply let her, behaved much the way Ingrid's husband did in moments like these. It left Ingrid waiting for the blow that would follow. The blow that would send her flying until she hit something solid that would knock sense into her.

But the blow never came. Reese simply took her blows, and this let Ingrid believe maybe Reese did know, or could.

"I let him have her. I didn't know, and then I found her like that. I should never have let him have her. He never lets me have anything to myself. He spoils the things I love, always he spoils them."

"You loved her?"

"Of course. I wanted to tell her. How could I know? You think it was from lack of love? She's the one didn't love me."

"Nina didn't?"

"Oh, Nina, she had others. She made that very clear."

"And your daughter?" Reese asked, catching on.

"What?"

"Had others?"

"She was a child."

"But did she?"

"She didn't tell me. She wouldn't tell me things, anything. It doesn't mean I didn't try to know. Ask her father. Oh, he assumed there were others. Don't you see? That was the trouble. There wasn't this trouble when she was small. It was all right then. There weren't these terrible scenes.

"But then, well, they grow up, don't they? And all the trouble begins." Ingrid was sitting on the bed now.

Reese sat beside her. "What kind of trouble?"

"The screaming. She didn't know how to be quiet. I knew, but she didn't. I thought she would. She was such a quiet baby, such an easy baby. I didn't . . . I wasn't prepared. And, by then, I was so worn-out. He'd long since lost interest in me. I didn't just . . . it just happened, began to happen. He picked her instead, and she put up a fight. She's more like him, you see. Not like me. She was never like me. She never much liked me.

"I knew it wasn't right of me. I tried to help her, but they were impossible to get between once it had started."

"Once what started?"

"The fights, and then I don't know. She'd storm out. It always began at dinnertime. After a while, we couldn't keep help, and I'm not good at fixing meals. I thought if I could just fix a nice dinner. But I never managed this. I came to know how bad it would be by how many times he sent me back to the kitchen for something I'd forgotten to put on the table. I'd pass in and out, bringing these things, and they'd begin arguing. And before I knew it, she'd've stormed up to her room and he'd've gone after her."

"And what would you do?"

"Clean up. As I said, we had no help. There was no one else to clean up."

"So they'd be upstairs?"

"Yes, that's right."

"And you'd be in the kitchen?"

"Yes."

"And you could hear them?"

"At first, then not so much. We have a large house."

"So you'd do the dishes?" Reese asked, incredulous by now, trying hard to wrap her mind around the unfathomable.

"Yes, someone had to."

"You didn't ever go upstairs?"

"Once or twice. A few times. Partway. I'd get to the landing. I could never get beyond the landing. Some nights I'd just sit there on the landing. Stay the night there, but it'd just make him angrier, make things worse.

"I didn't ever again after he threw me down. He found me there in the night and threw me down. And our hallway, our entryway—at the foot of the stairs, it's all marble. Beautiful really. Not that new shiny kind, not black. It was very old, nearly white with swirls of gray, a star pattern in black and white at the center, under the chandelier. When we still had parties everyone would comment on it. Say how lovely it was."

"Were you hurt?" Reese asked, fighting to maintain an even keel, keep the woman talking.

"Hurt?" Ingrid asked.

"Yes, when he threw you down the stairs."

"Well, we struggled. I fell. Yes, of course, it hurt."

"But did you need a doctor?"

"One came the next day. I thought I was all right, just bumps and bruises. But my collarbone had been broken."

"Did you tell the doctor what happened?"

Ingrid laughed—a scratchy, mournful sound. "Oh, no, seriously. You think that would be possible? Our doctor's an old friend. A friend of my husband's. There are dozens like him out there. They understand their job. Who pays the bills. They're not so stupid as to make things difficult."

Reese changed tacks, asking now, "How old was she?"

"What?"

"Your daughter, when all this started. You said they grow up and the trouble starts. How old was she?"

"Oh, I don't know. This went on for some time."

"But when it began?"

"Eight, I suppose, nine. Too young for school, to be sent away to school, though I planned that. I did that. But, of course, by then it was too late."

"Too late how?"

"The accident."

"What accident."

"My daughter died."

"Your husband . . ."

"Quieted things down. Made them go away. Except they didn't. Not entirely. Not for me, or for him either, given his behavior, though it wasn't something we spoke about. We used to talk. He was a charming man at one time. When I met him he was quite dashing. And in those days I had a certain appeal. He was not my only suitor, but, well, he persisted. And my father liked him very much. I don't think my mother would've liked him, but she was long since gone.

"In any case we married. And for a time it was glorious. But he soon tired of me. People do. And once my father died we had no need to maintain the pretense of happiness."

"Why?"

"The marriage, I suppose it was always an arrangement, though I didn't think so at the time. I'd convinced myself Gabriel cared for me, that I cared for him. It did seem that way once. But my husband and my father—joining their money, their business interests—I came to see what the marriage was really about. I know it seems rather Byzantine but these things do occur. They still occur."

Reese struggled to keep pace. All this information came at her like a flood after a drought. The preceding dry spell made it difficult to absorb. "Your father's business?" she asked, simply to keep Ingrid going.

"He began with fertilizer. I know it sounds somewhat comical—cow dung and all. That is how my grandfather started. But in my father's day fertilizer became pesticides, chemicals. And Gabriel, his interest was pharmaceuticals. It was all in some way related. They faced similar obstacles, perhaps. A merger—from the start this seemed inevitable. But Gabriel did not want to be my father's partner, or anyone else's.

"So he waited. He's an extremely patient man in some respects. And when my father died . . . I was an only child. All of it went to me. Or, to us. I signed whatever papers my husband put before me. I never quite followed it all. And from my mother, I'd learned not to question my husband's business. She never questioned my father. At that time a woman's questions were considered unseemly. I suppose it's all a bit old-fashioned but this was how she raised me.

"Later I learned not to question, well, anything he did."

"Because?"

"His temper. He learned to control it. Or appear to, and I learned not to incite him."

"But your daughter?"

"Yes, well, she never learned this. As I said, I tried to help her, but she'd have none of me. She had her own temper, much like his. She questioned him relentlessly, though unwittingly. She didn't understand what she was poking around in. But she wouldn't stop poking. There was no stopping her."

"At eight?"

"Yes. She was headstrong, and very beautiful. She looked older and spoke of things as if she were grown-up. She engaged him in a way I never could."

"How old was she when she died?"

"Oh, by then she truly was grown-up. I'd sent her away to school, but she hadn't lasted there. She'd started trouble there, too, so she came home again."

"She started trouble?"

"Yes, you understand: the usual things for a person that age. Drugs, boys. I wanted my husband to make it right with the school. Give some gift that would allow her to stay, but, of course, we were at cross-purposes. He wanted her home. And she wanted this as well. I think she got into trouble in order to come home. Her face that day I left her there—she looked at me as if I'd betrayed her. I'd tried to protect her, in my way, but she simply wouldn't allow it.

"Once she'd come home again—it wasn't very long then."

"How did he do it?"

"Do what?"

Reese searched for the right words. Ones that would implicate without scaring the woman off. "How did it happen?" she asked, then forced herself to use Ingrid's word. "The accident? How did it happen?"

"In the usual way."

"Usual?"

"Yes, well, as I've described: a loud fight. Them going upstairs. And him coming downstairs again later. That piece wasn't usual. I was sitting in the living room. Doing nothing, really. Waiting for . . . I don't know what I was waiting for, but I do remember the sensation of waiting.

"He came in looking a way I hadn't seen in many years. He looked quite young and helpless. For a moment he did before turning his back to me. He fixed a drink and sat down. And though I didn't want to, I couldn't not go upstairs.

"I looked into her room, but she wasn't there and so I went to our room. I tried to clean her up, take care of her. I didn't understand yet. I couldn't, you do see, don't you?"

And Reese nodded her head while the rest of her went the other way, was shaking, too. Shaking with anger. With wanting to seize this woman and throw her against the wall. She stood up. Walked a few paces away, put her back to Ingrid as if this could keep the woman from seeing her anger.

"What happened next?" Reese asked, still standing, but now facing Ingrid.

"She wouldn't wake up. I couldn't make her wake up. I thought she'd taken some drug again. I tried to pick her up, make her walk because, well, that's what you're supposed to do in those situations. But she wouldn't come around, so I took her into the bathroom. She was so very heavy, but I got her into the tub and ran cold water.

"He must have heard this because soon he was there, too. I asked for his help, because it was slippery and she was so much heavier than I'd imagined. I was on my knees beside the tub and she still wasn't waking up. She looked blue in the light there and I grew very afraid for her.

"I asked him to help me. And he crouched beside me. He reached out his hand. But it was to hit me. I didn't understand. I tried to stop him. I tried to hit him, but I'm not a strong person. I'm not physically strong. He hit me again, and then I hit my head. Things went, not black, but gray, gray and blue, and then black.

"And then he was over me. I don't know how much later this was. But he was holding a washcloth to my head when I woke up and I thought everything must be all right now, it has to be. But, of course, it wasn't."

"Your daughter?" Reese asked.

"She wasn't there anymore. He'd moved her, I didn't know where yet. But he had me get pulled together, pull myself together. And when they came, when the police came. She was in her own bed. And there were drug things around. And now it was an accident. Nothing in question."

"And you?"

"What?"

"You said nothing?"

"There was nothing to say. The police out there, they're like the doctors. They understand what not to question. My words would've been quite meaningless."

"But you didn't try?"

"With him there?"

"You were afraid of him?"

"I wanted it to be as he said. What I knew? Already it began to seem . . . fantastical. And the doctor had been called. My husband suggested sedation and he obliged. If I were to have begun ranting? They still put women like that away. Surely you see that people like us don't cooperate with the police. The police cooperate with us, with men like my husband."

And Reese did see this now. Saw it not as abstraction, but as something concrete. Something that could still trap a woman. Had certainly trapped this one. After all, they were having this conversation in a cell.

Reese sat down again. She felt a strange appreciation for this woman, who, this time, had called the police herself. From here she asked, "How did you call us?"

But Ingrid didn't seem to understand.

Reese tried again. "How is it you called the police today?"

"I didn't quite know I had. That, too, seemed fantastical. Like something I wished to be true, and then was, when you all appeared. But I grew afraid again. Of what I had done. Afraid of this happening." With these words she raised her hand, made a small gesture to her surroundings. "But this time I couldn't not . . . I'm not an unfeeling woman."

"I know that," Reese said.

Ingrid remained silent a little longer before saying, "There, now. I expect you've gotten what you came for, yes?"

"Yes," Reese said. But she lingered. She stayed, even though she'd had her fill of this. She got to her feet and Ingrid did, too.

But still Reese waited. She waited until the woman spoke again. Until she said, "Well, then, good night, Detective."

But as Ingrid turned away, retreated deeper into the cell, to the bed and the corner, Reese asked one last question. "How old did you say she was?"

"What?" Ingrid asked from the shadows.

"Your daughter? How old?"

"Thirteen, fourteen perhaps by then."

And hearing this Reese called for the guard, then quickly left the cell.

Twelve   Gabriel Santerre and Tom Burns sat in Santerre's study, ensconced in large leather chairs that were comfortable from use, burgundy in color. They discussed the events of the day. Santerre had his feet on a heavy wooden coffee table, a cigarette in one hand, a glass of scotch in the other.

Burns sat a bit more primly, feet on the floor, sipping his drink. He refrained from smoking, a habit he was trying to give up.

They'd finished with actual business, had completed their discussion of details. And so, having moved on from there, Santerre asked, "Is my wife . . . comfortable?"

"No, I wouldn't expect so."

"I don't want her to suffer unnecessarily."

"I understand, but her discomfort is quite necessary for the moment."

"Would it be imprudent for me to visit?"

"That would depend upon the degree of privacy we could secure. And, to a certain extent, on what you hope to accomplish. If the desired outcome is intimidation, I believe there's little need for that. If you wish to achieve another result, then the considerations are, of course, quite different."

Santerre remained silent, did not reveal his intent. Another cigarette was smoked before he spoke again. "I believe I would like to see my wife," he said finally, in a way Burns would not question. He would simply arrange for Santerre's desire to be fulfilled.

"Oh, and Tom . . ."

"Yes, sir?"

"I'd like to review those files myself. Just leave them on the desk, on your way out. And find out where that lawyer came from. I want to know who she is, and how my wife found her."

Burns got to his feet. He gathered the stack of files from the coffee table—files obtained from One Police Plaza, though each contained supplemental information. Information culled and collated by those on Santerre's payroll, or his balance sheet. Hard to find anyone who didn't work for him or owe him. The favors had come in steadily all day long, and most came of their own accord. They'd needed to call in very few. Burns placed the files neatly on Santerre's desk, and then left.

Gabriel Santerre smoked another cigarette and finished his drink before he got up. He went first to the bar. Then, with a fresh drink in hand, he sat at his desk. He leafed through each file, though only one really captured his interest—Caroline Reese, detective first grade, now here was some interesting reading material.

Gus Miller had secured the surveillance. It hadn't been easy but he'd eventually found the right man—Kayson, who'd taken early retirement to pursue a business venture that had quickly failed. Possessing experience and in need of cash, Kayson was a good choice. And he'd grown up forty miles north of the town, so he had some knowledge of the geography.

Against his better judgment, Miller had accompanied him. This was how he found himself, late at night, parked in a car near Carver's driveway. For hours now the two of them had observed no movement whatsoever.

The lights in the house had switched off. Soon after, small lights came on, illuminating the driveway. Evenly spaced, painted a dark green, they looked like miniature lighthouses, or odd-shaped bird feeders. They were quite inviting, though no one had taken the invitation. Miller, however, had counted them, or tried to. He kept getting to fourteen, seven on each side, before the driveway hooked left and then came back right again, affording a view of the garage, and the car, also dark green, still parked.

He'd begun his counting game some time ago, resorting to it when he and Kayson had run out of conversation. But now this game had abandoned him, too. He was left with his own thoughts and his thermos of coffee, both making him feel perfectly out of place on this quiet country road.

He half-expected the local police to cruise by and question their presence. And though he'd spent some of the long silence inventing responses to this event, it hadn't happened. A good thing because he'd been unable to devise a believable explanation.

Giving up this concern, he began thinking of Reese. How from the start this case had inflamed her, and how this had the unpleasant side effect of reigniting the dismal torch he carried for her.

It wearied and discouraged him to suffer these feelings again. Especially as he'd believed they'd been extinguished, once and for all, finally snuffed out by their one attempt at a date. His attempt, really. Reese had thought it just another night out together. She'd been visibly startled upon arriving at the restaurant he'd picked, discovering the candlelit table.

It had ended in laughter—hers, genuine and affectionate; his, feigned and anxious. They'd muddled through the awkward days and weeks that followed, finally returning to something near normal that saddened him.

So here he was, through no fault of hers, spending a night wrapped in one of her hunches. Hunches that infuriated him when they were wrong, but were too often right, and so could not be ignored.

That this one might be coming up empty? He disliked the satisfaction he felt. The way he'd begun practicing the exact way to throw it in her face. An attempt to make her pay for all the things she'd put him through, except she hadn't. He'd done these things of his own accord, and felt worse for knowing this. He would've preferred that easier place where he could believe she was actually at fault for his faults, for his feelings.

"You think we should pack it in?" Miller asked.

"Let's give it a bit longer," said Kayson, who had the incentive of pay for his hours.

Reese went to the morgue. The sleepy night man nodded at her badge. He recorded the time, handed Reese his clipboard, and watched her sign the log sheet, blank until now.

"Quiet tonight," she said.

He nodded again, said only, "You want 216."

"Thanks," she said, but he didn't reply.

Reese pushed the swinging door. She liked the feel of the room's cooler air, especially after the damp heat of

Ingrid's cell. She made her way down the squeaky floor. Found the number quickly, and opened the compartment.

Always this simple action had given her pleasure. The solid feel of the handle, the predictable noise it made when she pulled it, the smooth chrome, all of it reminded her of affable things—deli freezer cases, ice cream trucks, Eleanor's restaurant-quality refrigerator. These sensations and associations were not things she would ever have told anyone.

Here alone, she savored it all a bit before the room's empty echo reminded her where she was and what needed to come next. Pulling the tray, always the fear it would stick. And that unmistakable odor, too heavily masked to be absent. The overcompensation of disinfectant only making it more noticeable. Reese began to unzip the bag—one not so different than that golf case, just roomier, a different color. Reese unzipped it slowly, drew it open gingerly. And then she looked.

The girl did look different. She did look dead this time, right from the start. And this time she looked so very young. Reese shivered a little. But for this she blamed the room— its temperature, all the stainless steel surrounding her. She pushed away those last words of Ingrid's. Except she couldn't quite accomplish this, not entirely.

She settled for trying to determine what bothered her more—how young the daughter had been or that Ingrid didn't seem to know her exact age. But as Reese weighed these two choices, the third one emerged. The real one. What Ingrid had said with such aplomb. "Oh, by then she truly was grown-up." These were the words Reese took home with her.

Thirteen   Reese arrived early, but Miller was there already. He looked tired. She recognized his clothes from the day before, and so she got herself coffee, wondering whether or not to ask. She decided not to because she had an agenda, one she presented as soon as she sat down.

"I want to go back out there."

"Where?" he asked without enthusiasm.

"Carver's."

"I've been out there. All night."

"What? Couldn't you find anyone?"

"Oh, I found someone. And I've got her phone records."

"And?"

"Came up empty, empty all around."

"Is someone there now?"

"No. We stayed until four. She wasn't going anywhere. It didn't seem smart to stay parked there in broad daylight."

"She didn't go anywhere?"

"No."

"I've got to get back out there."

"Why? I've gone along so far but I don't think this is going anywhere. She's a dead end."

"No, she's not, but she could be."

"Huh?"

"I went to see the wife last night. She gave him to me. Gus, he killed their daughter."

"What?"

"Years ago. Had it covered up. We've got what we need now."

"On her say-so?"

"Why would she lie?"

"Because she's in a cell about to go somewhere less pleasant."

"No, she's not lying. And Carver will corroborate. I just need to go out there again—with this, with what I know now."

"You're reaching."

"No, I'm not. Hey, what's gotten into you, anyway?"

"Oh, I don't know. Just a night in a cold car with cold coffee."

"Well, why don't you spend today checking out those nice warm houses. Find someone who knows the girl. Find out where Santerre fits there."

"Better than going back to suburbia, I guess."

Carver hadn't slept. She'd turned out the lights, spent the night curled on the couch fighting urges. She knew better than to call, better than to try to leave. They knew more than they let on. The cops did. The woman did, anyway. She couldn't place what they knew. Couldn't clearly remember the exchange.

Now that it was morning she felt she had to leave, had to go anywhere else. But the places she frequented all seemed pointless and wrong. The alternative—to wait and see who came to her? This seemed, well, stupid came to mind.

She showered and dressed, was on her way to her car

when another car came up the driveway. The detectives' car, but the woman was alone this time. Reese, that was it, her name. Carver turned her back to the approaching car, opened the door of her own car. She was about to get in when the detective pulled up alongside her.

"Ms. Carver," she said. And the girl turned toward her, saw Reese moving quickly, and then, there she was—right in front of her, blocking her.

"You back for more?" Carver asked, struggling to maintain control, to stay cold.

"Just a few more questions. Can we go inside?"

"I was just going out."

"Well, can I drive you somewhere? We could talk in the car."

"I don't think so, Detective. I think we're finished."

"I think there's more you want to tell me."

The detective had taken her hand, then taken the keys from her. She'd gained the advantage so quickly Carver couldn't see how this had happened. How she'd let it happen. She looked at Reese, wanted to handle her the way she had the day before. She knew she was weaker than she had been, but Reese behaved differently, too. She presented more of a challenge. And Carver, accustomed as she was to meeting challenges, could not meet this one.

She wanted to account her weakness to lack of sleep. But it wasn't that. She was used to that. It was where her mind had taken her once she'd succumbed. Once she'd accepted that her customary escapes were unavailable. Her thoughts had run back to Ingrid.

Whenever Carver went back, was taken back, to the time she'd spent with her, with them, she became like this—

fragile. Susceptible to any promise of care or rescue. And so she stood, here and now, vulnerable to the belief that Reese offered these things. That Reese could deliver—could deliver her.

But then the detective said, "I want to help you."

The words laid it all before Carver too sharply. And they sharpened her because she'd heard words like these many times. And she'd seen them turned against her again and again, until finally she'd arrived at a place where her belief in people and their words seemed her ultimate flaw.

"Oh, so now it's me you want to help?" she said, and tried to snatch her keys back.

But Reese held them just out of reach. She said, "Why don't we go inside."

"All right then, Detective. Have it your way."

They walked toward the house. Carver a little ahead, too aware of Reese behind her, pushing her, herding her. When they reached the door, she stopped. "Can I have my keys, or did you want to open the door?"

Reese handed her the keys. Carver thought of making a run for her car, but it would've been futile. She knew she was incapable of quick movement. That Reese would overtake her. And then what? The thought of this almost made Carver try it because she envisioned the detective stopping her physically, holding her back, holding her. It seemed more and more to Carver that her entire life revolved around the simple desire to be held—a notion she had as much trouble tolerating as escaping.

She unlocked the door, and Reese followed her in. They were soon on that same couch together with Carver waiting for what came next. No longer even pretending to know what that might be.

Reese said, "I want you to come back with me."

"Oh, so now you're arresting me?"

"No, no. I want you to talk to Ingrid."

"That's your job."

Reese stayed silent and the silence made Carver uncomfortable, so she spoke again, but differently. "Do you know what he'd do to me?" She asked this quietly, as if asking herself and not Reese. "Do you?" she asked again, this time meeting Reese's eyes, but seeing only determination there.

"He won't know. We can arrange it. We can protect you."

"My God. You really believe that, don't you?"

"Yes."

"Do you have any idea who you're dealing with? Who you want to get me messed up with? You have no idea."

"I have every idea. And I know you want to help her."

"You think I'm still so foolish as that. Is that the impression I've given?"

"I don't think you're foolish at all. I think you want to see him pay. For what he did to you. What he did to her. I think you want to see him pay for that girl in the hotel room. And the daughter. It was the daughter, wasn't it?"

At this Carver got up. She fetched a pack of cigarettes from a table across the room, lit one with her back to Reese. She remained standing that way for some time.

Carver turned. "So they did her in a hotel. What was it? The Four Fucking Seasons?"

"It was the daughter," Reese said again, but this time not questioning.

Carver nodded.

"Why don't you come and sit down, Ms. Carver."

"Oh, so we're back to formalities now. A new game today." But she relented, did as Reese requested.

"Tell me about the daughter."

"I have nothing to tell. She was gone long before I came."

"Then tell me about you. When you came."

And though Carver had spent the night there, with it coming at her over and over, she could not make it intelligible, not even to herself. And so without the desire to withhold or become harsh, she became both, not wanting anyone to know how it still made her, still ran her life. She believed if anyone knew the power of those months to incapacitate her, they would see her as weak, or crazy, or both. And that then they would most certainly take advantage.

Reese said, "Nina . . ."

Carver looked at her fiercely, beat back tears. Began to get up, but collapsed partway through the motion. Sat listless for a time before speaking, before saying, "You don't understand what you're asking."

"Tell me, then."

"I need you to leave."

"I don't think so."

"Why can't you just leave me alone? Leave me out of this?"

"I can't do that. You're already in this. You're in this whether you help me or not. You want out of this? You help me. Help me to help you."

"That's a crock and you know it. You're in this to use me. That's the only place I fit." And when Reese said nothing to this, Carver continued, "Would you at least admit it."

"I know it looks that way," Reese began. "I know you have no reason to believe me. But you don't know me. Give me that much. I'm only saying we want the same thing here."

"And what's that again?"

"To put him away. To keep her from going away for what we both know he did."

"You can put her away till the end of time for all I care."

"Maybe so, but that only solves half your problem."

"My problem? I didn't have any problem until you showed up. I was just fine until then."

"You expect me to believe that? I can see you're far from all right."

"Oh you can, can you?"

"I'm not stupid either." Reese grabbed Carver's wrist, turned it so the marks along her forearm showed. "You think I'm so stupid or unobservant, I didn't see these yesterday? But if you're happy. Are you happy, Nina? Is that what you're trying to tell me? That I've come here and disrupted your idyllic country life? Tell me you're happy, Nina. Then I'll leave."

But Carver couldn't say those words, or any words, because she'd begun sobbing, or something like it. Sounds caught in her throat, the tears caught behind her eyes, and there was Reese's hand, still fast to her wrist. The detective not giving an inch today, and Carver liking her this way. Carver flirting now with the notion of placing belief in someone one last time and having it turn out differently.

"Think about it," Reese said, releasing Carver, getting up to leave.

"Don't go," Carver said.

"I'm leaving. It's what you want, right? You can either come with me or stay. Those are the choices."

"I have to think."

"You can do that by yourself."

"Can you really protect me? From him, I mean."

"We'll do our best."

And though this likely wasn't good enough, Carver felt herself acquiescing. She got to her feet and followed Reese to her car. And she got in because while the place Reese would take her might not be pleasant, it would at least be different. And because this detective seemed like the only solid thing she'd had to hold on to in years.

Fourteen   Reese parked under the station house and took Carver up the back way. She left her in an interview room on a different floor and put a uniform at the door. Then she climbed the extra flight to the squad room.

Miller was on the phone when she came in. She acted easy, got herself some coffee, shuffled some papers, but as soon as he hung up she said, "I've got Carver."

"What?"

"Downstairs, I've got her. I want to put her together with the wife, fast. Before she gets twitchy on me."

"Bad timing."

"What?"

"The husband's here."

"Where?"

"There," he said, pointing to a room behind her. "With the wife," he added.

"How?"

"What do you mean how? A fucking conjugal visit. How's that?"

"Get serious."

"I've been serious."

"Have you talked to Eleanor?"

"I've got a call in to her, but she hasn't called back."

"No, she's in court. Does she even know about this?"

"I doubt it. He came waltzing in. They brought her up. He had it all arranged."

"His lawyer here?"

"Made a brief appearance then left, but I'm sure he'll be back for escort duty."

"What's the lieutenant got to say?"

"Go in and ask him yourself. Me, I've been ducking him. I'm not asking to lose my pension on this."

Reese got to her feet, though uncertainly. She stood there wavering—physically listing between the glassed-in office and her chair. Gravity won. "Shit," was the only thing she had left to say.

Gabriel Santerre stood, looming at the head of the table. Ingrid sat at the foot, as disheveled as he was immaculate. He'd been working her for some time, was saying now, "Darling, you know as well as I how this happened. You brought this on us. We could've taken care of it ourselves. But you had to go and make this mess. Bring these . . . outsiders into our lives. Now Tom and I are left cleaning this up. We've arranged a nice place for you. You won't be there long. Then it will be like it was again."

Ingrid had spoken very few words. To this, she said, "I won't go there."

"You've given us very few alternatives. You've made things quite difficult."

"I'm not the one who . . . ," she said, without finishing.

"Who what?"

"You know as well as I do."

"And now you know, too, the price of this kind of stunt.

Have you any idea what's required now? Of the disruption? The cost of this?"

To this Ingrid said nothing.

Reese weighed her choices: there was Carver downstairs; Harris; and her first choice, the one she took. Without another word, she got up and went for the interview room. She knocked quickly, then barged in.

Santerre wheeled on her. "This is a private meeting," he said.

"Oh, excuse me," Reese said. "My mistake." But before exiting she caught Ingrid's eye. She hoped it would be enough.

Back outside now, it was her lieutenant's turn. Her trick had not escaped him. He stood at his door. She went in without making him ask.

"Interesting," he said, as she sat down.

"Someone's got to do something," she said before tempering herself. "How long has he been at her?"

"Oh, I'd say about an hour."

"And it'll just go on until he's had enough?"

"She agreed to see him. She wanted to see him. But I'd say they're just about finished."

Reese followed his gaze, saw Burns come in. Then watched him go into the room. Not long after, he and Santerre left. "I'll take her back down," she said. And before Harris could say anything else she'd made for the room again.

Once inside, she tried to gauge Ingrid, determine how much damage control was required. She appeared surprisingly strong. But Reese couldn't be sure. She said, "Are you all right?"

"Yes, Detective. I'm quite all right."

And she did seem to be. Reese took her arm, took her out of the room and down the stairs. She paused after the first flight. She wanted to put her with Carver, but it was too big a risk. She couldn't let this moment's impatience undo everything she'd accomplished. So she kept walking her, kept walking down until they were underground, back in the cell.

Before leaving, she asked, "Did he hurt you?" not sure quite what she meant by the question.

But Ingrid seemed to. She said, "Not so much. Not in the way he can."

Reese said, "You're sure you're all right?"

"Yes, I'm quite all right, Detective."

"Okay, then," Reese said, and went back upstairs to Carver.

She found her shaking. Shaking so hard, Reese said, "Look, are you needing something? I should've asked before. How long can you go?"

Carver looked up blankly, so Reese said, "I could get something for you. If that's the trouble."

"No. Look, I've made a mistake. This is a mistake. I have to get out of here. I have to go home. You understand me?"

Reese understood all too well. She'd brought her in too quickly. Too much, too fast. And now? Reese needed a way to stake the ground she'd won. "Okay," she said, "I understand. Look, I'll take you back."

"I'm not sure that would be wise," Carver said.

Reese could see the girl struggling to make her voice work. Make it function properly. And she was still shaking.

But it didn't look like the shakes that need dope. This looked like plain old fear, terror even.

Reese said, "I think you'd better let me drive you."

Carver gave Reese one more hard look before she let go. Before she gave in and said, "All right, but just to the train."

In the car they were quiet. Reese kept herself still. She would not push this young woman over the edge she was clearly so close to. Carver was the one who finally spoke, asking, "Have you ever killed anyone?"

It wasn't an uncommon question. Cops got asked it all the time. Girl cops especially, Reese believed. That image of a woman with a gun—so compelling, so intriguing and loathsome all at once. But Reese knew Carver'd asked this from an uncommon place, not for the usual reasons. Because of this she gave an unusual answer. She said, "Twice," when always, ordinarily, she would say once.

"How did it feel?"

"You can't know until you've done it. It's not something you can describe."

"Tell me."

Reese weighed this. How much to tell.

"I won't tell you there's no satisfaction in it. But it's fleeting. No matter what your reasons, no matter what makes you do it, the price is always there. And part of that's the hurt afterwards. You think it'll undo the hurt but it makes it bigger. There's more to get over, not less."

Reese wasn't talking about her on-the-job shoot. She couldn't make that plain to Carver, though it felt peculiar to be telling her things she'd told no one else.

"Have you ever been hurt?" Carver asked next, and then added, "I mean, shot."

"Yes."

The answer hung there between them. She didn't volunteer anything more, and Carver didn't ask. They'd arrived at Grand Central. The horns and hordes encroached. Carver's hand was on the door handle, but before she could get out, Reese took her other hand. She said, "We'll try this again."

She felt the hesitation in Carver, felt the tension in the woman's hand as she tried to pull away. Reese held on, waited for Carver to either pull free or not.

Carver let go of the door. She sat still a minute. Looked at Reese, who said, "Tomorrow? We'll try again?"

Carver nodded and then she was gone. Out of the car in an instant. Reese watched as she maneuvered the crowd and disappeared through the doors.

Fifteen   Reese went back to the station house, back to the squad room. Gus Miller sat there still, still at his desk. As she sat down, he said, "Everything taken care of?"

"For now, anyway. You get hold of Eleanor?"

"Yeah, she's on it, but she didn't sound too happy."

"We need to get someone on Carver."

"I thought you had her."

"Had to take her back. I just dropped her at the train. We need someone watching her."

"Well, I'm not spending another night out there. I'm telling you, there's nothing to see. She's not going anywhere."

"Well, what if someone's coming to her? Gus, you saw how close that was. I told her I could protect her from Santerre, and then he's here. I'm lucky they didn't meet on the stairs."

"Yeah, well, they didn't. He didn't see her, so stop worrying it. Besides, if you'd just told me you were bringing her in, I could've told you he was here."

"I didn't want to risk it."

"Well, look where that got you."

"Yeah, I know. You're right." She shoved some papers around on her desk, then said, "You really think there's no point watching her?"

"I can't know that. But with what you're saying about

her, she sees a car at the end of her driveway, it might really spook her. Make matters worse."

"Yeah, that's true. We still have her phone covered?"

"Yep."

"Guess that'll have to be enough. Pathology come back yet?"

"Nope, jammed up."

"So, you want to check out the houses?"

"I suppose it's next on the list."

Carver's train ride had passed in a blur. The cab home, too, seemed faster than usual, faster than she wanted it to be. Once in her house, she felt it worse, felt it more—the fear.

She wondered if she should've stayed. If she'd made the wrong choice by coming back here, coming home. Home didn't seem the right word anymore. Maybe it had never been the right word to call this house, though it did contain her things. But none of them felt like hers.

She roamed the rooms, picked up objects and put them back down. She knew she ought to shower, change clothes. She didn't want to do these things. Flirted with the idea of forgoing them. Just this once, not bothering. Showing up as who she was now instead of who she'd always been. Though she was still unsure what that meant. She felt as if she'd only just discovered who she was. And she'd discovered, too, that she didn't know this person who'd stayed under wraps for so long.

She resisted the urge to account her changed thinking to Reese. Didn't want to get caught in that idea—so wrong-headed, so old. Something she simply couldn't afford because she'd have to pay for it herself.

Still, she couldn't just go on with her life either, not as it had been. So the rest of it, this evening at least, would be going through motions. She would accomplish the things she needed to do in a mechanical fashion. But it was six o'clock already. She was running late.

Reese and Miller headed out, headed east—over to Madison Avenue just above Fifty-seventh. They parked near the most likely house—the one Reese's hunch told her to try. Rarefied, discreet, it catered to scions. And it was less than ten blocks north of the Ascot Towers.

It was early evening, just after six, so the odds of catching a few girls on their way in was good. They waited and they watched, and Reese took the first one they spotted.

She approached the young woman carefully. "Excuse me," she said, putting herself between the girl and her destination. This one looked like a college student. Probably one of the many who needed money for tuition—recruited from Barnard no doubt, or some other expensive school.

"Excuse me," Reese said again, "do you have a minute?"

"No, actually, I don't," the woman said, stopping only when she caught a glimmer of Reese's badge, shown in an instant and then put away.

"What do you want?" she said now.

"You know a girl named Julie? Jewel maybe?"

The woman backed away from the question, went silent and colder. Reese kept pressing until the woman said, "Look, I don't need this, I don't need trouble. What I need is to get to work, so unless I've done something, that's where I'm going."

Reese let her pass.

By seven a car had pulled up outside Carver's house, was waiting for her. She grabbed her bag, trying to hurry, but unable. Sluggishly she went out the door, locked it behind her. She got into the car, limo actually, and nodded to the driver. But she made none of her usual small talk. She didn't even attempt it.

The driver left her alone, left off his banter when she'd given back only a few murmurs. She'd forgotten the damn drug. Forgotten to take care of that at home as she usually did. Wondered for a moment whether to just go without. But the risk of that went way beyond reason.

"Nothing personal, Tony," she said as she pressed the button, raised the smoked-glass window that separated front from back. And then the digging into her bag, finding the preloaded syringe she always carried. Then finding a vein. Choosing one on her thigh because if she couldn't go without, she'd at least slow the delivery.

This drive, too, would be shorter than she wanted. She left the partition up. Worried some for Tony's feelings, but needed more to be alone than to take care of him. She thought about drugs—the summer before when people'd begun dropping like flies. Just a few snorts of that high-test stuff then on the market had put them down for good.

So she'd made the trek. Gone to the old haunts, asking for it by name: Blue Heaven. And all this time she'd kept what she'd bought. It remained sealed in a clear glass vial, hidden beneath the false bottom of a desk drawer. Her own cyanide pill waiting for the right moment.

As the car approached her destination, as another graveled driveway crunched under tires, she wondered if this time had finally arrived. Blue Heaven—she laughed at this sick joke on herself. The stuff fed her in copious amounts? The stuff in endless supply? No matter how much she took, it certainly would never take her there.

It was nearly half past seven. For well over an hour, Reese and Miller had alternated, getting nowhere—stonewalled by women who knew their rights and their minds. Now, another one appeared. She looked younger, and though it was Miller's turn, Reese said, "Let me take her."

"Sure," he said.

Reese approached the girl quickly, all too aware of the attention she and Miller might've already attracted. She hurried up the sidewalk. Wanted to get the girl as far from the doorway as possible. Reese moved fast but not fast enough to start the girl running the other way, tip her off. She'd set her sights on this one because she looked like the dead girl, looked not unlike Carver, but younger—unquestionably underage.

She caught her at the corner, hustled her around it.

"Hey what're you . . ."

"I need to ask you some questions," Reese said, one hand still on the girl, the other on her badge.

"Oh, look, can you give me a rest?"

"Do you know a girl named Julie? Jewel?"

The name was all it took. The girl tried to shake loose, saying, "Leave me alone, all right?"

"No, it's not all right."

"Then, not here. Not out here."

Reese looked around. Took the girl to the nearest place, a coffee shop a few steps down the block. She put her in a booth and sat opposite.

Carver got out of the car. She gave a nod to Tony, who'd just sit there waiting for her. It was all so predictable.

She went to the door, which, of course, was unlocked. She went inside, locked it behind her. Her shoes, her heels, scraped the marble floor with a sound that hurt her teeth and announced her arrival. But he wouldn't come to her, she'd go to him. All scripted, played over and over for years.

Carver went to the study where he sat waiting. She took her seat on the leather couch. After appraising her, he would fix her a drink. A drink she never wanted because it just didn't go with the stuff always already inside her. Still tonight when he put it in front of her she drank it, all of it.

They didn't speak. They'd been beyond words for years, but nonetheless they usually engaged in some banal chit-chat. Not tonight. Tonight he simply handed her another drink, and when she'd finished that one, too, they retired.

"So tell me about Julie," Reese said to the girl. "Is that her name?"

"No, it's Jewel. Where is she?"

"You don't know?"

"No."

A waitress came to the table. Reese ordered them both coffee. Then she began again. "She's dead . . . What's your name?"

"Cherise."

"Well, look Cherise . . . That's your real name?"

The girl looked away from her.

"We'll get to that, then. For now tell me what you know."

"Nothing. I don't know anything. I didn't know she was dead. She was fine."

"When? When did you see her?"

"Before the weekend. Must've been Friday. Busy night. That's when he comes in."

"He?"

"Yeah. He's a regular. Well, not exactly. He's not like the others."

The waitress brought the coffee. Reese asked the girl if she was hungry, but she shook her head. When the waitress had left again, Reese crouched forward, toward the girl. It looked like she was going to get a lot more from her than she'd ever imagined.

"So tell me about him," she said to get Cherise started again.

"Don't know much. I never went with him. I just kept getting called in every week. Or, every time he showed."

"Called in to work?"

"No, I always work. Called in. You know."

"No, I don't know."

"To the office. Or the back. It's kind of an office, the room back there."

"So what would happen?"

"There'd be a few of us. Not too many. He'd pick."

"And he never picked you?"

"No, okay? He never did."

"I didn't mean . . ."

"Yeah, sure you didn't."

"He picked Jewel?" Reese asked to get back to more neutral ground. Using the name again worked.

"Yeah."

"He picked her just last Friday?"

"Yeah."

"Had he picked her before?"

"No, he never takes the same one twice."

"So you'd been through this before."

"Always a bridesmaid . . ."

"Would you rather be dead?"

"Jewel's really dead?"

"Yes."

"We thought she got lucky. When she didn't come back we thought she'd got lucky. Found one."

The room they went to, the master bedroom, wasn't entirely the same. It had been redecorated many times in the years that had passed. And that his wife never appeared during their times together made for some difference. Usually these things gave Carver enough distance from what had come between them all before.

The wife certainly couldn't appear tonight. That was for damn sure. But tonight she was there anyway. Carver couldn't shake her, couldn't put her away in that box, that place in her mind where she'd kept her for years.

The sex she provided had become as mechanical as the rest of the routine, though usually she didn't notice this either, didn't show it. Didn't notice that maybe he felt that way, too. That he might be growing as tired of their arrangement as she was. This thought came to her so crisply it scared her. It came as he did—by his own hand and not through her, not inside her. This, too, was not new. But, like everything else, it seemed clearer. So all of it, every moment of it, looked uglier to her than she'd let it look before.

He didn't tie her up anymore. Like the absence of his wife it was something she'd insisted upon when they'd struck this bargain. When he'd come after her again. Found her, just when she'd thought she'd escaped him.

Now there was only one escape she could think of— Blue Heaven. She did have that. That vial was hers. She had that waiting at home. The only thing in that house that truly belonged to her. The rest of it all on loan. Waiting to be repossessed. Waiting for a night like tonight when it would feel over to both of them.

Reese kept at Cherise. She said now, "So the others came back?"

"Yes."

"What did they say about him?"

"They wouldn't say anything. The older ones would tease them, but they wouldn't talk."

"Tease them how?"

"Oh, you know, call them chosen things, boss's pet, stuff like that."

"So he was your boss?"

"No. Our boss—he's something very different. Not exactly mister suit-and-tie. Charges us back for everything from toilet paper to stained sheets. And what do we get? Protection. That's a laugh. Supposed to watch what comes in. All they care about is how much money. Act like they're doing us some big favor."

Reese let her go on like this, complaining. When the rant had finished, Reese asked, "How'd you get into this?"

"The usual way. Couldn't go home, needed money."

"How old are you?"

She looked away. Said to the wall, "How old do I look?"

"I don't know really. You tell me."

"Too old. I look too old. That's what they tell me. Be worth more if I looked my age, had less wear and tear."

"Tell me."

"Fourteen, okay? Satisfied?"

This stopped Reese, or at least slowed her. She'd figured seventeen. "You had to leave home?"

"Yeah."

"You can't go back?"

"No fucking way. Hey, you're not one of those, are you? You're not one of them who'll try and make me go back?"

"No. I'm investigating a homicide. That's my interest here. It doesn't go any further."

"No, of course not. Why should anyone be interested . . ."

"Hey, hold on there. You help me with this, maybe we could do something."

"Save it. Believe me, I've heard it all."

Reese believed she had. And she couldn't not think of Carver. Of the things she hadn't asked her, hadn't even asked herself about her. Now Reese wondered how Carver had wound up with Santerre in the first place, where she'd come from.

Usually Reese's job insulated her. She'd see snatches of people's lives. Like this girl tonight, she'd get just a little glimpse. She'd never have to see the whole of it. Instead she'd move on to the next—the next ugly piece of someone's life gone momentarily wrong. That's how she worked it. But Reese couldn't work this case that way.

Now that he'd finished, he rolled away from her. He'd remained dressed, another habit of his, so all he needed to do was zip his pants. From his pocket he took his own vial and a small penknife. The knife was the only new thing, so startlingly new Carver looked for other differences.

She found only one—his belt, crackly new. Smooth and shiny, burgundy. She always avoided looking at his belt, so it wasn't surprising she hadn't noticed before. She could surmise what had become of the old one.

She watched him dump the contents of the vial across the glass-topped bedside table. Saw him cut it and arrange it with the knife. She wanted to ask about the knife, but stopped herself. She liked the silence between them too much. Instead she contented herself with his actions, observing them closely.

Once he'd arranged the cocaine, he took out his little gold tube and began taking the stuff. He always waited until after. Another way to remind her he needed nothing. And he never offered her any. Their fondness for opposite drugs just another thing that made them such a good match.

Reese forced herself back to the matter at hand, to the girl before her. "Okay, then," she said, "tell me what you've heard about this man. Do you know his name?"

"Not really. They make some joke about it. Call him San-teria, after some voodoo thing. Like if you go with him you get the zombie hex."

Reese felt a shiver. She'd been stirring her coffee, just to do something with her hands. Now she put her hands under the table. She didn't want Cherise to see the shake in them.

But she'd noticed. She'd seen something, because she said, "What?"

"Nothing, go on, tell me what you mean. Why they say that."

"Well they do come back all narced out. They don't say much or do much for days. And they get coddled for a while. Get the easy ones. Me, I get the fucking coke tricks. The ones who go at you for hours. Right? Because I'm young, but can't ever get chosen. And I'm not one of the older ones. I guess you could say I'm valued for my endurance."

"You're jealous of them?"

"Who?"

"The ones he picks."

"Don't know. Never thought about it much."

"Come on."

"Yeah, well, they do get babied while the rest of us do the work. That's why with Jewel . . . ," her voice went funny, caught and quivery. "I thought she was all set up."

Carver had lingered longer than usual. She put herself into motion because she didn't want to hear the sound of his voice. She got herself up and out of that bed. But she dressed with the weight of her new knowledge slowing her movements. All these things she now saw so sharply made her dull and tired.

Once dressed, she left him there still rutting around with his coke, made her way downstairs. In the entryway, atop a large black chest—one imported from Hong Kong ages ago, according to Ingrid—sat her envelope. She snatched it up, stuffed it into her bag, and went out to the car.

Tony'd left the partition up. Kind of him, she thought. Kind of him to leave her alone with her thoughts, which now again came to Reese. That the detective would appear the next day—knowing this could get Carver through the night, give her someplace else to go, other than that vial in her drawer. She looked at the limo's digital clock. The one set into the paneling before her—a spark of red in the dark. At least doing him hadn't taken long, but it meant that much more time until morning.

"Would you recognize him?" Reese now asked Cherise.

"I suppose so."

"Do you know what his involvement is? Why he rates such special treatment?"

"Money, right?"

"Is there more to it?"

"You'd have to ask someone else."

"You sure about that?"

"Look, I only know what I hear from the others. I haven't exactly been there for ages. Some of them, it's their whole fucking life."

"But not yours?"

"I do things, other things."

"Like what?"

"I don't know. Stuff. I make a lot of money, you know. I don't come cheap."

"Even with all the chargebacks."

"Yeah, well, look it up in goddamned *Fortune* magazine. I'm making a fucking fortune compared to most."

"Most?"

"Yeah, well, you for instance. What do you make?"

"Enough."

"I bet it isn't half what I take. I've got plans, you know. I'm not going to be there forever. I'm not like some of them who just say that, and then stay and stay. I've got savings. I've got it stashed. Tax-free, you know?"

"So you're just in it for money?"

"That's right."

Carver said good night to Tony, then made her way into the house. Her body was gummy and heavy, but her mind moved about quickly, restless and edgy. She went to the desk, opened that drawer, took the envelope from her bag, and tossed it in.

She hadn't turned on any lights but the moon was bright. The envelope glistened. Bright white against a backdrop of green because usually she opened the envelopes, poured cash into the drawer. Usually she enjoyed this. And she used to enjoy her trips to the bank, watching the accumulation.

She hadn't made that trip for some time so there was a lot of money lying there. More than enough to abscond, to simply vanish. Plenty more in the bank. But underneath these schemes lay another false bottom. Each time she pictured herself on some beautiful beach, finally free, he intruded.

The vision only seemed real once he'd appeared in it,

spoiled it. That first part remained beyond her imagination. She could only make it gauzy—filmy and flimsy. But upon his arrival, every detail came along with him. He'd stand over her, smiling. Say he'd had his own banking to do, the offshore kind. Remarkable, he'd say. What a pleasant coincidence, their meeting again.

Carver slammed the drawer closed. Went upstairs and undressed. Took a long shower before crawling into bed. And when sleep still eluded her, she pulled her bedside drawer open. Found yet another syringe. Put herself down with this one.

Reese had finished with Cherise, gotten all that she could. They left the coffee shop together. Reese handed her card to the girl as they neared the corner. Then she watched her make her way down the block, across the next street, then halfway down and through the doorway. The one Gus Miller still watched.

Returning to the car, she tried to sound enthusiastic. "Pay dirt with that one," she said.

"Yeah? What'd you get?"

"Santerre comes in regularly. Picks girls out, young ones. She knew the dead one. Hell, she could *be* the dead one."

With these last words Reese couldn't maintain her excited charade. She went moody and quiet.

Miller said, "So you want to try a few more?" he asked.

"No, let's head back."

Sixteen   The two detectives stayed silent as they drove back toward the station house. But when they hit Fifth Avenue, Miller asked Reese if she wanted him to drop her at home. She took him up on the offer, knew he could tell something was bothering her, though they still didn't talk much on the way downtown.

He pulled up in front of her building, then said, "You're worried about her, aren't you?"

"What?"

"Carver, you're still worried about her. Look, why don't I go out there now. Anything happens, I'll call you."

"But you did it last night. If anyone should have to, it's me."

"Yeah, but you're working her. She sees you, you're screwed. She sees me—hell, she won't even recognize me. Worst case, she'll think Santerre's got someone on her."

"Think he does?"

"I don't know."

They sat there a little while longer. Then Miller said, "Go on in, get some sleep. One of us needs to be fresh in the morning."

"Okay," she said but she didn't move yet. "You're sure you want to do this?"

"Yeah, I'm sure."

"Thanks," she said, and then she got out of the car.

He stayed parked until she'd gone inside. And she could see him sitting there still as she waited for the elevator. She waved to him when it arrived, then stepped inside.

Tired as she was, Reese still felt restless. She kept pacing around her apartment. She knew it was Carver. That, really, she'd wanted to go out there herself. But Miller was right. And she knew he'd call if anything happened.

She ran a bath because usually this worked to slow her mind. Getting into the tub, dipping down into the water, she felt her shoulders drop. Her thoughts dropped, too. Went farther down, farther back. First just to earlier that day, driving Carver to the train. Carver asking her about killing, what it felt like. A cryptic conversation. Cryptic on her end.

Once her thoughts landed here, she couldn't linger in the tub. She got out, dried off, and went to bed. But she lay awake still thinking too much. And when she finally drifted into sleep it was fitful. She woke again and again, not remembering what had woken her, but knowing nonetheless. Knowing that nights like these were always about Frank. Whenever she woke sweating and shivering, it was Frank.

After three rounds of this, she got up and fixed herself a drink. A large one in a glass Eleanor had given her. So taking her drink to bed with her, she began thinking about Eleanor. How she'd helped her after Frank. How Eleanor had almost helped her get over Frank. Almost but not quite, so he was still always there. And the questions Carver'd asked had brought back the dreams. The drink finally put her back to sleep, but it didn't put away those dreams. Frank coming at her in another coked-up rage. Her not so clean herself— coked-up, too, when she'd grabbed the nearest heavy object.

They'd taken their jobs home with them, become only their jobs. They weren't the first undercover narcs to drop down too far. But that he'd wound up dead, while she'd wound up promoted, then transferred—Eleanor had called it justice. But even she didn't know that if Reese had been tested that night she'd've come up dirty.

So it'd been put away. An internal affair in every sense. Kept quiet. And Reese had kept quiet, too, because no one had asked her the right questions. No one had wanted those answers. No one had wanted to hear them, except Eleanor. And any time Eleanor had gotten too close to those questions, those answers, Reese had pushed her away. And then Eleanor'd left. She'd left the whole fucking system. All of this months ago, but still dogging Reese.

Everyone had said fresh start, new precinct, shiny new shield. Everyone had said put it behind you. And she'd tried to, though she'd refused counseling. They'd forced it on her, of course. Mandatory under the circumstances. But she hadn't really gone along. She'd shown up for the required number of sessions, but that was that. And so it still came at her. At night, he still came at her. Frank did.

She woke once more with that tingling sensation. The one she hated most of all. The satisfaction she'd mentioned to Carver, always followed by horror. And the horror so disquieting because she could never quite determine if it was real. Whether the true horror came because maybe she wasn't so horrified. And everyone working so hard to convince her it'd been justified—justified homicide—that only intensified her conundrum.

This hadn't been any clean kill. It'd been terribly messy inside and out. Frank lying by the side of her bed. His head caved in by the marble brick, the one that still decorated her bedside table. His blood everywhere. On her clothes, sticky on her hands, on her face, in her hair.

But her first kill'd been clean. Though that time, too, she'd been left sticky with blood, her own blood. Shot in the line of duty. The neatness of that first kill helped them tidy up the second one. They all wanted to believe the best of her, it seemed. And they were all ready to believe the worst of Frank. The Internal Affairs Bureau's inquiry went by like some small formality. Reese believed Eleanor must've pulled every string she had for IAB to go that easy. And when it was all over, that hideous night became just more grist for the mill. A real cop's cop. That's the reputation she'd won. She'd earned the kind of respect most women could never hope to achieve on this job.

And the promotion had worked. It had bolstered her belief in the system, the department. All its finer points had worked in her favor. The department's capacity to quietly make things go away had taken care of her. Kept anyone from looking too closely. She'd believed the system had kept her from being sent up on murder. That, and Eleanor's skill at working it. So she'd believed in it all. The fraternal order, her acceptance into the boys' club—she'd questioned none of it. At least not aloud. She'd thought the system worked well enough. Until she saw Santerre work it.

Once more she drifted to sleep, only to be jolted awake again. This time she bolted—out of bed and into the shower. And then she killed time, doing little or nothing, pacing around. She killed time until she could go back to work.

WEDNESDAY

Seventeen   Reese arrived at the station house so early the night shift hadn't even left yet. She spent a half hour or so trading stories with those guys. It kept her from going down to the basement, checking on Ingrid. Or calling Miller.

Soon enough he came in, looking rumpled, but cheerful. He'd brought Danish and coffee, good coffee from the place she liked. They'd barely sat down when Reese said, "So?"

"Nothing. She stayed in all night."

"You get any sleep?"

"Not much."

The phone rang, and Reese picked it up. It was Eleanor.

"Look," her friend said, "I've been able to keep the wife with you the rest of the week. I told them it'd save money. Save them trucking her back and forth. They always like that one."

"That's great," Reese said, but the tiredness of her voice didn't match her words.

"I'll be in today. Will you be there?"

"In the afternoon. Come in the afternoon. I'm bringing Carver back in."

"Back in?"

"Yeah, I tried it yesterday. Tried to put her and Ingrid together, but it was too soon. Might've worked but I didn't expect the husband-and-wife reunion."

"That wasn't my fault."

"I didn't say it was."

Eleanor didn't say anything to this, so Reese said, "Can we make sure that doesn't happen again?"

"I doubt it. Not if she wants to see him. That's your end. If you can convince her not to see him—"

"I can try."

"So when will you be back with Carver?"

"I'll call you from the car."

"So, I'm just supposed to sit around waiting for your call?"

"Aren't you pretty mobile? I mean, those Wall Street guys gave you that cell phone . . ." Instantly Reese regretted saying it. She said, "I'm sorry," before her friend could say anything in return.

"Well, I've got paperwork, anyway."

"I'll call you as soon as I've got Carver here," Reese said, and then she hung up the phone.

Miller said, "So, you're heading back out there?"

"Yeah. I don't suppose you feel like coming along?"

"And I don't suppose you want company."

The sound of a car woke Carver. She went to her window, still grogged from the drug but fearful nonetheless. The sight of Reese getting out of the car didn't still her fear. She pulled her robe from the foot of the bed. As she made her way to the stairs, she drew the robe around her, huddled inside the soft folds of antique silk.

The bell hurt her ears. She went downstairs with the single intention of stopping the noise—let that goal block everything else.

When Carver opened the door, Reese asked, "Did I wake you?"

"No, no. I'm just running a little behind schedule."

"Well, I can wait out here while you get ready."

"No, it's all right. Come inside."

Carver ushered Reese to that same room, that same couch. Then she said, "I'll just be a minute," and retreated quickly back upstairs.

In the shower she wondered at the stupidity of letting a detective roam her house. She realized she didn't care what Reese found. Realized she wished there was something to find. Something concrete that would put an end to this existence of hers without her having to do anything. Not exactly a fairy-tale ending, but an ending. Prison had become a place that seemed safe to her. A place he'd want her to be, and so would let her be.

She turned the faucets, let cold water douse her before she stepped out of the shower. But she still didn't quite feel awake. She put her robe on again and went to get dressed.

As Carver expected, Reese did roam around downstairs. She went from room to room, looking. The large kitchen appeared little used. The dining room, the same. The whole downstairs seemed that way, save the room she'd started in and now returned to. There were some signs of life there at least, but nothing that told her anything much about Carver.

Reese now stood near a heavy desk. She was about to open a drawer when she heard footsteps. She faded away from the desk, met Carver as she came into the room.

"Ready?" Reese asked.

"Guess so," Carver answered.

. . .

Reese drove the dirt roads in silence. She didn't want to initiate conversation. She wanted Carver to do it. Reese wanted Carver to volunteer the things she'd never asked her—where she'd come from, how she'd wound up with Santerre, with Ingrid. Reese didn't want to have to ask, she wanted Carver just to tell her.

But on the highway, closer to her own turf, Reese simply began talking. She said, "You nervous?"

"Huh?" Carver asked.

"Seeing her again. Ingrid. It's been a while, right?"

"Yes, quite a while."

"Seven years, isn't it?" Reese asked.

"Oh, I don't know? Did I say that?"

"Maybe she did."

"Oh."

"You must've been young then. What: thirteen? Fourteen?"

"I guess so. I don't remember really."

"Really? Young to be on your own. I'd think you'd remember."

"Well, I was messed-up then."

Reese stopped herself from saying "And you aren't now?" Instead she said, "Parents?"

"What?"

"Your parents?"

"What about them?"

"They just let you?"

"Let me what?"

"Fend for yourself?"

"I suppose. They weren't around much then. Better all around that way."

"So, there was trouble there?"

Carver said nothing.

Reese figured she was on the right track—getting Carver angry tended to yield the most information. "Big trouble?" she asked now, glancing over at her.

Carver shrugged. Then she said, "How would I know? I don't exactly carry a measuring stick."

"Looks like it to me."

"Like what?"

"Like big trouble," Reese said.

"I don't think about it. Can't go home again and all that."

"You want to, though?"

"What?"

"Go home?"

"No such place."

"You went home with him."

"Who?"

"Santerre. He took you home with him."

"That was a mistake. I knew better."

"But you stayed there. Because of her?"

"She . . . Money, you know, money. They paid well. He did."

"I see."

"No, no you don't. You don't see at all."

"Sure I do. You needed to make a buck, support yourself. I get it. Hey, money's important." Reese still had half an eye on Carver. She saw her lip quivering. It was working.

"No," Carver said, "that's not it. You don't understand."

"I just said I did."

"But you don't. He wasn't there all the time. She was . . . she was nice to me."

"Oh? How's that?"

"I don't know. She just was." Carver's voice had become very young. But as if she'd caught this herself, caught herself, she said harshly, "That was my 'Are you my mother?' phase."

"What do you mean?"

"You know, like the book. That kid's book. Never mind."

"No, I know it. Dr. Seuss, right?"

"Yeah, I guess so. That one."

Carver's face had flooded red. Reese didn't want to lose her, so she quickly said, "I liked that one. I remember it." But when Carver still didn't come around, Reese said, "Hey, it's okay."

"What is?"

"You can talk to me. You can tell me."

"Tell you what?"

"Whatever it is you need to say."

But the words just stayed there, suspended between them. Carver had closed off and so Reese let her be for now. She didn't say anything more until they were nearing the station house. Then she gambled. She said, "Did you have a mother?"

Without pause Carver said, "Not so's you'd notice."

Reese had forgotten to call Eleanor. She circled the block to make time for the call. Eleanor said she'd be there soon, as soon as possible.

"Who was that?" Carver asked.

"Mrs. Santerre's lawyer."

Reese thought she saw Carver tremble so she added, "An old friend of mine. No one you know."

Carver went back silent while Reese continued circling, buying time. She didn't want Carver sitting too long in some interview room. She would avoid the mistakes of yesterday. The ones she could avoid. Springing Carver on Ingrid would either work or it wouldn't.

Eighteen   Reese was still circling the block when Carver asked, "So are we doing this or not?"

"Yep, right now." Reese said, turning into the station house this pass, taking them underground to the garage. She brought Carver in the same way as yesterday, brought her to the same room. From there, she called upstairs, and Miller picked up.

"Eleanor here yet?" she asked.

"Right here. She just came in."

"Send her down to me, will you?"

"She's on her way."

Reese waited for Eleanor to come in, and then made the introductions. She couldn't read Carver's response. She'd gone shaky again, so shaky, Reese asked, "You up to this?"

"Can we just get it over with already?" Carver said.

Reese left her with Eleanor. Went downstairs to get Ingrid. The woman looked worse for wear, seemed to have lost some of the strength she'd had the day before.

"I've got someone upstairs wants to see you."

Now Ingrid went shaky. "My husband?"

"No, someone I think you want to see."

"You'll forgive me, Detective, if I don't take your word on that."

Reese wouldn't relinquish the surprise factor. She said, "Just come with me."

Ingrid complied. The guard was there by Reese's side, but she waved her away. She took a firm hold of Ingrid's arm and escorted her up the stairs. With each flight, she felt the woman's reluctance increase. By the time they reached the right floor, began making their way down the hallway, Reese felt as if she was dragging the woman.

And when Reese opened the interview-room door, when Ingrid saw Eleanor first and then Carver, the woman dipped so far down Reese nearly had to catch her. But she recovered herself, and then she moved like air. Floated, it seemed, across the room to Carver, who was quickly on her feet.

"Ah, look at you," Ingrid said. "You're all grown-up now."

Reese shot Eleanor a look, but she was watching the women. They faced each other, nearly circled each other, before they came together. Carver went to this woman's arms like she'd never left them. The two melted into each other in such a way Reese felt embarrassed watching, intrusive.

And Ingrid kept murmuring, "Look at you," again and again until the words assumed a life of their own.

Carver didn't speak. She didn't say a word. She just held Ingrid, let Ingrid hold her. Ingrid stroked her hair, kept murmuring to her, cooing. Still the same words, then saying, "Ah, Nina, I've . . ." But with this, Carver sharply and suddenly broke away.

Reese blocked her path to the door. Carver tried to push past her, was yelling now. Yelling, "Let me the fuck out of here."

"It's all right," Reese said, "I'm here."

"Let go of me," Carver said. And she struggled fiercely before she gave way, finally collapsing into Reese's arms.

Reese held her, while looking past her, first at Eleanor, who remained seated, impassive, and then at Ingrid, who looked stricken.

"Sweetheart . . . ," Ingrid began, but she said nothing more than this, had nothing to follow it with.

Carver wheeled in Reese's arms, turned on Ingrid. "Don't you start that with me," she screamed at her.

Reese still held her, held her by her wrists, held her hands behind her back to keep her from going at Ingrid. But Carver, half-crazed by now, yelled at Reese, "Let go of me. Get your fucking hands off me."

Reese didn't let go, she held fast and waited while Carver kept ranting, at her, at Ingrid. And through it all Eleanor sat calmly, observing, until Reese said to her, "Get her the hell out of here. Take her next door."

Eleanor acquiesced. She got to her feet and escorted Ingrid out. Once this was done, Carver went slack. Reese let go of her wrists. She still stood behind her, unsure whether to try to touch her or just let her alone. She let her be, because touching her seemed impossible.

Carver went for her bag, which sat atop the table. She fished it robotically, retrieving a syringe.

"Whoa," Reese said. "You can't do that here, you can't do that in front of me."

"Then leave," Carver said as if it were just that simple.

"Hold on," Reese said, moving toward her now, taking the hand that held the syringe. "You can't have that in here."

"Yesterday you offered it to me."

"Not that. I said I could get you something. Not that." As she spoke, Reese unclenched Carver's hand, worked her fingers under the girl's. "You can't go running for this all the time."

"Oh, no?"

"No."

"Why the hell not?"

"Because it isn't working."

This seemed to catch Carver off guard. Her fingers loosened and Reese took the syringe, but then gave it back. "Put this away and sit down," she said.

Carver gave her one last fierce look, then she threw the syringe back in her bag, but she stayed standing. She looked unsure what to do with herself, with her body. She staggered, listed one way, and then another before Reese caught her. Until Reese held her, and then she began to cry.

In the room next door, Eleanor Coffey sat across from Ingrid. They had said very little. Ingrid found herself uncomfortable with the silence and so finally broke it. "I never meant to hurt her," she began. "It wasn't my intention. I never meant for things to get so out of hand."

Eleanor said nothing to this, forcing Ingrid to continue or endure more silence. "He hurt her very badly."

"*He* did?" Eleanor said.

"Oh, I see, you think I'm at fault for what he did. Everyone thinks that sooner or later, I suppose."

Reese let go when Carver pulled away, when Carver plunked herself down in the nearest chair. Reese waited for the girl to collect herself before she asked, "Should we give it another try?"

She expected Carver to resist, but the girl said only, "You keep her away from me. You keep her hands off me."

"All right," Reese said. Then she poked her head out the door, had a uniform retrieve Eleanor and Ingrid.

Following Eleanor into the room, Ingrid looked strangely calm, or wary, Reese couldn't be sure which. Eleanor took her same chair, retained her same manner. Ingrid seemed uncertain where to put herself, so Reese led her to a chair across the table from Carver—one next to Eleanor. She, herself, took a chair at Carver's side.

Surprisingly, Ingrid broke the silence. She said cryptically, "How is my husband?"

Carver met the question evenly. "Same as ever," she said, keeping her eyes fixed on Ingrid's.

A charge ran through Reese. She looked to Eleanor for grounding and her friend returned the look, but Reese couldn't tell if Eleanor shared her surprise. She felt unaccountably betrayed—felt Carver had betrayed her.

Reese worked to get herself back. She tried to see this new information as something good. Something she could use if she could hold on to Carver's confidence. But now Reese felt she had never won Carver's confidence. Not if Carver'd withheld this—had been with Santerre this whole time. And Reese had never sensed it. It had never occurred to her, not even an inkling, she'd completely missed it, and this most of all left Reese shaky.

Carver and Ingrid still held steady, still held each other's eyes. Ingrid spoke again, "So you remain satisfied with the arrangement?"

"Yes," Carver said, though her voice quavered slightly with this single word.

Reese wanted to make this a way in, but she had that same feeling of intrusion. That she and Eleanor should leave these two alone and see what came of it. But she knew they would not behave this way if left to themselves. That this was part stage show, at least for Ingrid. Reese could hear it in her measured tones, feel it in her determined composure.

Reese knew Ingrid meant to prove something with this exchange. And though she couldn't place the why of it, she understood it was somehow for her benefit. That the woman's agenda involved her in some way. Reese knew Ingrid had not done this unwittingly. She clearly meant to expose Carver, expose her to Reese.

"Well," Ingrid said now, "as long as you're happy."

With this, Reese heard her own words to Carver, or ones like them. And she saw Carver's face trembling. Saw the young woman's hand move mechanically toward her bag but then draw back. And then Carver looked at her, at Reese, a pleading look.

In return, Reese said, "Maybe we've all had enough for today."

Now Eleanor shot her a "What are you doing?" look. Reese ignored it. But Ingrid wasn't finished. She said, "I suppose it's easier for you now. Now that I'm here."

But Carver had gone mute. Her breaths came short and ragged. Her hands, with nothing to do, simply shook. She clasped them together as if to still their movements, but then the shivering took hold in her arms.

Reese looked back and forth between the two women. First to Ingrid's stony precision, and then to the mess she'd made of Carver. And still Reese had the uneasy and certain belief that Ingrid was doing this for her. But just when she'd become wholly convinced of this, fixed on this, Ingrid moved beyond it. Moved to a place where Reese didn't exist and couldn't follow.

"Yes, I expect it's easier. Easier for you to know I can't possibly intrude—"

"No," Carver said, the word coming as an exhalation.

"Oh, come now, Sweetheart. Let's not play—"

"No, it isn't easy."

"No?" the woman said now, cagily gauging, seizing this.

"No."

"Oh? I thought I was the one made things so difficult for you. The one you wanted away from. Remember? You do remember."

Carver was still struggling. "Stop it," she yelled.

"I can't. I tried to, but you wouldn't let me. You wouldn't let go of him. Remember?"

"That wasn't it. You know that wasn't—"

"How was I to know this?" But with these words Ingrid's hold began to slip, too. Her voice went from precise to edgy. Edgier still when she continued. "Go on, tell me how I should have known. What I should've known."

"You knew. You knew all along."

"What?"

"What I felt. What I wanted."

"And I didn't feel—"

"No. It wasn't real."

"Don't tell me what's inside—"

"Nothing. There's nothing there. Nothing inside you."

With these jabs from Carver, Ingrid lost her footing. She looked bruised and tumbled. A single tear ran down her cheek to settle near the corner of her mouth. She moved her hand to brush it away, but this only spread it out. Her jaw glistened. The bruise there shone—yellowed, nearly green beneath the fluorescent light.

Now more tears, but still slow ones. Ingrid struggled to talk through them, to keep her voice steady. But now she'd begun pleading. "You know that isn't so. You can't believe that."

"Can't I?" Carver shot back. And when Ingrid couldn't answer her, Carver pounced. "What was I to believe then? You're the one who left. You're always leaving." But with this Carver lost her grasp, seemed no longer to be talking to Ingrid or about her. "Always, you're leaving me," she said, and by now her own tears had started again.

"I tried to keep you safe," Ingrid said. She, too, seemed to be talking to someone else. "You wouldn't let me. If only you'd let me. Can you still not see who he is? Who I am?"

Carver shoved her chair back. Reese grabbed her arm, but the girl pulled away. Then they were both on their feet. Carver, again trying for the door, Reese again blocking her. Now it was truly over. Reese knew she couldn't push Carver any further. Not without losing her entirely.

She resorted to anger—the one thing that worked with both these women. "You sit down," she yelled at Carver, then turned to Ingrid. "And you shut up."

She called in a uniform. Told him to take Ingrid downstairs. And she told Eleanor to go with them. Made sure Eleanor would stay with Ingrid until she'd finished with Carver.

Through all this Ingrid had stayed in her chair. She still sat there. The uniform and Eleanor each took an arm, virtually hoisted her, and then walked her. As the three of them left the room, Ingrid looked back, her gaze trained on Reese.

When they'd gone, when the door had closed behind them, Reese stood a moment looking after them, after Ingrid. Reese stood there, very still, determined to collect herself before turning toward Carver.

Reese's first question came evenly, quietly, but her voice was cold when she said, "You keeping any other secrets?"

Carver still cried, though she did this so silently that when she began to speak, or tried to, the words wouldn't come. She reached for her bag again. Reese stiffened in response, but Carver retrieved only a handkerchief. She hid her face in it, covered her eyes.

The sight of this softened Reese more than she wanted. She took the chair next to Carver's and said, "Come on, now. It'll be all right, but you need to tell me if there's anything else."

"There's nothing else."

"You're sure?"

Carver nodded.

"So, when do you see him?" Reese asked.

"Whenever he wants me."

"So, there's no schedule to it?"

"No. How am I to know when he'd rather trip off with some girl to a hotel? Bring the wife along."

"So you really haven't seen her in all these years?"

"No."

"How'd you manage that?"

"Like she said . . ."

"What?"

"Ingrid," Carver said, spitting out the name. "Like she said: He and I have an arrangement."

"Why'd he agree?"

"He had his reasons."

"And they were?"

"Oh, look, it's a long story, a long time ago."

Reese left off this for now. "So what's the arrangement?"

"No wife."

"And?"

Here, Carver balked. She reached for her bag, but Reese shoved it away, then grabbed Carver's wrist.

"What else?" Reese asked, tightening her grip.

Carver said, "I don't let him tie me. I'm not so stupid as to end up like that one you people found."

Reese let go of Carver's arm. "What do you know about how we found her? Did he tell you something?"

"He didn't have to."

"But would he? Would he tell you things?" Reese asked, though she didn't like where her own questions led.

"Oh, I see," Carver said. "You want me to spy for you. Wires and tape recorders, is that the idea?" And now she was laughing—an odd, off-kilter sound. "Don't you people usually tape all that to people's bodies? Where would I put it?"

"That's not quite what I had in mind," Reese said.

Carver wasn't laughing now. "What exactly do you have in mind?"

Reese was slow to answer. Her mind had too clear an image of Carver with Santerre. But she pressed on. "There'd be a great deal of risk involved. You'd have to assess the risk you'd be taking. Whether that risk outweighed the possible outcome." Reese couldn't relax her words, knew she sounded like a page from the patrol guide.

Carver'd begun laughing again. "Like it hasn't been risky all along."

This sharpened Reese. "You didn't tell me. When I told you I could protect you, I didn't know you had this . . . this arrangement."

Carver quieted now. Softly she said, "I guess I thought you knew. Or you'd know. That somehow you'd just know and I wouldn't have to tell you. I didn't want to have to tell you. But I didn't want this. You finding out this way. With her in there like that. Her doing that."

"I know you didn't," Reese said.

They sat silently a little while before Reese said, "How did you know about that girl? That he'd tied her?"

"That's his way. That's what he lives for. That and all the wheeling and dealing. It's a life, I suppose."

"And your life?" Reese said.

"What?"

"What do you live for?"

"If I thought too much about that, I don't expect I'd live at all."

"Maybe it's the other way around."

"What?"

"Maybe if you thought about it, you'd have a different life," Reese said, fighting an all too clear understanding that this one had a death wish—one Reese didn't want a hand in fulfilling. "Look," she said, "I don't think you should go back out there. I don't think you should see him again."

"What? Don't you want to get the bad guy? Isn't that what *you* live for, Detective?"

Nineteen   Reese couldn't persuade Carver not to go back, but she did arrange to meet her the next day. And Carver agreed to let Miller drive her to the train station. While they waited for him to come down, Reese asked one final question.

"Have you been with Santerre recently?"

"Last night," Carver said.

"What?" Reese asked.

"Last night."

"What time last night?"

"I don't know exactly."

But then Miller knocked. He came into the room. Reese stared at him until he said, "Everything all right?"

"Yeah," she said, "just fine."

Reese let Miller take Carver, then she headed for the stairs, trying to believe there was some explanation why he'd said Carver'd stayed in all night—any explanation other than the one she was thinking. The one she couldn't shake as she hurried down the stairs, down to Ingrid. She'd just have to hope, just as she'd have to hope Santerre didn't already know she'd been meeting with Carver.

She'd hit the corridor. Slowed her pace as she neared Ingrid's cell. She paused, hearing Eleanor's voice.

"So, what's in it for you?" Eleanor was saying.

"Nothing," Ingrid replied.

"I'm supposed to believe that?"

"You believe whatever you want. That's what everyone does, isn't it?"

Reese motioned to the guard to let her into the cell. Once the three of them were in that small space, it became all too close—so close Reese couldn't read anything. Too many thoughts crowded her mind. And the light was so dim, both Eleanor and Ingrid blurred before her.

Then Ingrid said, "Come to rough me up, Detective?"

The words focused Reese because the impulse was there—to throw Ingrid against the wall, force things from her. But she didn't like that it showed.

"So, Mrs. Santerre," Reese began, "what else have you got up your sleeve?"

"As I told your friend here, there's nothing else. But she doesn't seem to believe me. Perhaps you could convince her . . ."

"Enough," Reese yelled, "I've had enough of you. You're standing in a goddamned cell with the only two people between you and a murder conviction and you still want to play games? You have fun jerking us around? You keeping more secrets just so you can put on more little shows? Like that one upstairs? What was that about? Putting Carver through that?"

"Believe me, Detective, she's no child. I don't know that she ever was one."

Reese saw it. A slight quavering ran through Ingrid as she spoke these words. She kept her voice steady but the rest of her wobbled. So there it was—the way inside.

"Is that how you sleep at night? By convincing yourself

she's all grown-up? That she always was? Even then? Huh? What was she, thirteen, fourteen maybe? And you? What? You just let him?"

"Why do you continue to insist that I'm responsible for my husband's actions?"

And, again, the woman's voice stayed steady, while the rest of her trembled.

"You were there, lady. You were there with that girl in that hotel. You were there with Carver. You were there the night he killed your daughter. What was her name? Did you even tell me her name? Or don't you remember? Don't you remember the names of the girls he kills? The girls you help him kill. How many names?"

"Lila," Ingrid said, her voice shaking now with the rest of her. "Lila," she said again, taking a small step toward Reese, but then veering off, finding her bed, settling there.

Reese turned away from Ingrid, turned to Eleanor, who said, "Caroline, why don't you take a minute. I'll meet you upstairs."

Reese didn't want to leave, but she relented. She kicked the bars to get the guard's attention, and then she was gone.

In her absence, Ingrid seemed completely limp. Eleanor just stood there looking at her, unsure what to do, how to mop up. "We'll need to talk more, Mrs. Santerre." It was all Eleanor could think to say before leaving. And she had no idea whether Ingrid had heard her.

Eleanor Coffey climbed the stairs to the squad room. She hesitated at the swinging doors, then pushed her way in. She found Reese at her desk, slamming things—the phone, files, drawers—anything in reach. She stood back, unsure what to do here, too. Finally she took Miller's chair, wanting the physical barrier of the desks between them. She didn't want this rage turned on her. "Caroline," she began. But Reese didn't seem to hear. "Caroline," she said, louder this time. "Caroline, stop it."

And Reese did. She gave one last slam to a drawer and then stopped, looked up and around her.

"What a piece of work that bitch is," Reese said, the words coming from under her breath.

"There's more," Eleanor said quietly.

"Oh, great. I can't wait."

"Not here. We shouldn't talk here."

"Yeah you're right," Reese said. "Let's get out of here."

Twenty   They went to Eleanor's. They took her car, staying silent during the drive. Reese had to stop herself from making snide comments about the Mercedes. Instead she tried to take comfort in the car. The way it smelled of leather, not new, but still there. She ran her fingers along the wooden dash. Eleanor had taste, Reese decided, trying to find anything nice to think.

At the apartment, Reese headed for the couch while Eleanor made the drinks. Once they were both sitting, Reese said, "So, what've you got?"

"Ingrid owns Carver's house."

"Jesus. Not Santerre? When'd you get that?"

"This morning. But there's more. She owns the houses. She owns the house the dead girl came from."

"How'd you get all this?"

"I called in some favors. Did some digging. My place of employment is not without its advantages."

"How many houses?"

"Half a dozen. All the same type of place, but spread around the city."

"Dates?"

"One after another. A year or less between each closing."

"Her own little empire. Anyone else involved?"

"Nope, she's the sole name on the titles. No syndicates, no attempt at disguise."

"Santerre'd have to know. You think they wanted to be found out?"

"Her, maybe. Him, no way. Though from what I've discovered, he seems to believe he's untouchable. Maybe he wants to prove it. And he may be right. Caroline, everyone's in his pocket, and not just in this city. I've looked into his company—"

"Harris told me. INISCO, right? Drugs, chemicals, that stuff."

"Yeah, that stuff. They call it Pharmacy to the World. The good life through pills and powders. Look for them dumping some FDA flop somewhere near you. Or, more recently, more accurately, look for them buying FDA approval. But the pharmaceutical arm's lily white compared to the chemical wing."

"Right hand gets the left hand what it wants . . ."

"And vice versa. Think Desert Storm. Think Iraq, pre–Gulf War. Think chemicals as in chemical warfare. Dousing people sick and dead in a variety of ways for a variety of reasons. Think PAC, think Pentagon, but most of all think profit. Profit and power."

"What I'm thinking is we're fucked. Thoroughly and totally fucked."

"Well, that is his other area of expertise. Caroline, no one wants him to go down."

"So his reach goes . . ."

"From sea to shining sea, and across them both. But our concern is much closer to home. You said it yourself."

"Said what?"

"That his story sounded like he'd had it ready for years. Clearly he planned, laid groundwork, prepared for this contingency. Probably why those titles are in his wife's name. A little extra insurance in the event he got caught. Make the frame on his wife hang just a little bit straighter."

"So what? He's just playing us?"

"What do you think?"

"I don't want to think what I'm thinking."

"Which is?"

"That I'm . . . that we're pawns in some game of his. That the whole damn bureaucracy's indulging his whims. I mean they throw something this scale into our little squad . . . Gus said it right from the start."

"Said what?"

"That if they threw us this big a fish, they either wanted it caught a certain way or thrown back. And Harris said it from the start, too. Said Santerre'd bought the mayor, had every city official on down in his hand. But then he tells me, go on out and try to catch the guy. That he'd clear my case-load. Gus's, too. He even warned me, said he couldn't stop what might happen if things went sour. Told me to warn Gus. So what's his angle?"

"Caroline, from what I've heard Harris is a career fence-sitter. Likes to pad his landing both sides."

"So he'll just keep feeding me rope until I hang myself with it?"

"Or until you make a collar from it. One that makes him look good. You been reporting back to him?"

"At first, though not so much lately. But only because I haven't had the time, and he hasn't been asking."

"Is Gus?"

"I don't know. I don't know at all about Gus anymore."

"What do you mean?"

"Last night, he said he'd go out to Carver's, keep watch on her. Tells me she stayed in all night. Then she tells me she was with Santerre. Tell me how to add that so he comes out right. And tell me how to convince myself Santerre doesn't already know."

"Know what?"

"About Carver's trips downtown. My trips out there. And now I've gone and sent her back out there. And Gus is the one I get to drive her to the train. Ellie, that girl . . ."

"What?"

"I asked her to fish for me. Ellie, she barely blinked. I think she wants to be next on his list."

"You can't stop that."

"Yeah, well, maybe not, but I sure don't want to put it in motion."

"He's had years to kill her. Maybe he wants her alive. Maybe he needs her. The wife certainly seems to."

"Or maybe he just doesn't want to give her what she wants."

Twenty-one   Carver stepped off the train and instantly she felt it. A dusky stillness reminded her of something she couldn't place, something she wouldn't remember. But when she saw the limo—his limo—waiting there for her, the memory was inescapable.

If she'd had any lingering doubts, the car's presence assured her he knew everything. And that he'd decided to raise the stakes.

She walked slowly to the car, nearly floated toward it. Once inside, she tried to affect calm. Over the years she'd repeatedly used this strategy. And always she'd achieved some semblance of composure. At least she'd believed she had.

But tonight even affectation eluded her. She tried to keep herself from trembling, but she did not succeed. And she was unable to still her mind, keep it from returning to the night he'd had her cut.

She kept her eyes straight ahead. Looked at the back of Tony's neck. Looked to him to afford some comfort. But this couldn't work because Tony'd been along that night. He'd had last crack at her. And he'd been the hardest to endure, though, over the years, Carver had convinced herself her difficulty with Tony had resulted from fatigue, the bruising she'd already taken, simple soreness—no more to it than that.

But these days Tony was easy to take. She wondered now if this was merely because circumstances demanded it. Because she saw him so often. Saw him all the time, but at least separated from her. Him always in the front seat, the glass partition available if necessary.

And, too, she'd convinced herself he'd had no role in cutting her. That he'd been unaware it was coming. As unaware as she was. And this was plausible, likely even, though she understood it was merely a function of his position. That he was a driver, not a hatchet man.

Still, he'd chosen to remain a driver. The other two were subcontractors, long since gone. Dismissed and replaced several times over, while Tony'd kept his job. So though he'd been in on the action that night, in her and on her, he'd never graduated.

She tried to return to the here and now. Did so fleetingly, wondering where Santerre would have her taken. What he had in mind. But whatever it was, she suspected she'd survive it. That seemed the ultimate insult. That he kept making her endure without reward, without rescue.

But now rescue had come to mean something else. And she could no longer persuade herself Reese had no place in this change. She thought of the detective busting in to save her from Santerre. Carver had finally to acknowledge the existence of this embarrassing wish, was no longer able to defend against it.

All her customary defenses seemed either inadequate or stripped from her. Taken away before she was done with them, before she'd found others to replace them. Even the syringe in her bag seemed bankrupt. Reese had shown her that: those simple words—it isn't working. They'd lodged in

Carver's mind. No lecture, no moralizing, just a statement of fact, indisputable fact.

She struggled away from these thoughts—tried to regain her former self. She struggled for breath, but the air was so thick it seemed to clot in her throat. And so Carver was left trying to swallow instead of breathe.

Reese left Eleanor Coffey's apartment in a state close to shock. She walked blindly, if purposefully, down. Occasionally she jerked her head back to search a cab, but if one appeared she found herself too slow putting up her arm.

So she just kept walking. She walked the eighty-five blocks that separated her Fifth Avenue apartment from Eleanor's. And the whole way down she kept flashing on Carver, Santerre, Ingrid—glimpses of Miller, of Harris. A long walk spent wondering what she was in for, and if she'd been unable to catch a cab because of where she would've asked the driver to take her.

Santerre waited in his study. He thought of his afternoon meeting with Burns. His attorney's plea that he keep quiet for a time—resist the temptation of public forays. He recognized the wisdom of this strategy, and so did not question it. What stayed with him was the language Burns used. Though Burns tried admirably to hide it, he always revealed a hint of distaste when forced, however obliquely, to discuss Santerre's predilections.

Santerre tolerated his attorney's behavior, knowing that, kept in the right balance, this aspect of Burns was what made him so good at his job. Santerre picked up the file Burns had delivered. He leafed through it, finding the information displeasing but, nonetheless, interesting. So his wife now, too, had a formidable attorney in her employ. Well, he'd deal with that easily enough.

Santerre tossed the file back on the coffee table and picked up his drink. One would have to look very closely, would have to be looking for it, to see that he gripped his glass a bit more tightly than usual, or that he extinguished his cigarettes before he'd finished them; that he rose from his chair more frequently, for ice, a splash more scotch.

Beneath this veneer of control, he seethed. His anger consumed him to such a degree that its true target was obscured. So hard to reach, impossible to reach, and so he'd sight the available one. The one he'd been using in his daughter's stead for years now. He needed her—needed Nina to provide this crucial service, and this, too, incited him.

As he waited for her, for Nina, his thoughts returned to the night he'd met her. That he'd found her so close to home still seemed miraculous. There'd been another ugly scene with his wife—commonplace back then, so soon after the accident. Ingrid had wailed at him. She'd reached a level of ferocity that no amount of sedation could contain.

That night she'd begun throwing things. Breakable things shattering against walls, until the disorder, the disarray, had become too great for him to bear.

He'd made for the door—glass objects flying at him, crashing near him, littering the marble hallway. Ingrid's aim was either off or precise because not a single one touched him. Finally a marble egg hit the marble floor. It skidded, then rolled—wobbled really, trembling at last beside his shoe. A brief quiet before the wail came again. "Bring her back," Ingrid had keened one last time before slumping to the floor.

And so he'd driven himself to the train station. He'd planned to spend the night away—a night off in a hotel, a quiet night alone to collect himself. And then he'd sighted her—Nina—clearly trolling the parking lot. She'd so resembled his daughter he'd cautioned himself as if against an apparition.

He'd approached her. Then quickly he'd taken her arm, the way he had so often with his daughter. He'd done this to convince himself she actually existed—flesh and blood, and not illusion, delusion.

She'd attempted coarseness. But he'd seen it didn't suit her. She hadn't yet learned to play this part, and so she was just right for the one he had in mind. In every way, she'd serve his purpose. The plan had already begun taking shape. And as he'd formulated it, his satisfaction had surfaced in a slight smile. "Bring her back?" He'd do just what his wife had requested. For the first time he'd do exactly as she asked.

As the limo hit the dirt roads, Carver, too, was thinking of the night she and Santerre had met. She had been working the parking lot. On this much they agreed. And he had seemed ghostly to her as well, coming it seemed from nowhere, taking her arm.

His grasp had been light, but well placed. He'd taken her elbow using not his hand but his fingers and thumb. His thumb and two, maybe three fingers digging into the joint in a way that made movement difficult. In this way he'd steered her.

They'd made no agreement, struck no bargain. She'd wound up in his car. She'd let herself be taken. As he'd turned up the long driveway to his house, she'd still wondered how she'd allowed it. And then she'd been led to Ingrid. Naively, stupidly even, she'd mistaken this for fate.

Santerre smiled slightly now, remembering the way his wife had gasped when he'd brought Nina into their house. Ingrid had stayed where he'd left her—crumpled on the marble floor amidst shards of glass.

As he'd brought Nina inside, his wife had stirred from the sound of the door, her head rising to greet them. Then the moment he'd savored in advance—her hand jerking to her mouth to trap the sound that had already escaped it.

Carver remembered the sound as well. Unearthly, ungodly even, it still haunted her. This sound more than anything else had sealed her in, fastened her to Ingrid.

This piece had no place in Santerre's plan. The moment would remain forever marred because the girl had disengaged from him. She'd gone so quickly from his side to his wife's, had crossed the hall to kneel by her side. And so he'd miscalculated. He'd believed that because Nina so looked the part, she'd play it.

.   .   .

Even now, Carver shuddered, remembering the sound and the stricken, uncomprehending look in the woman's eyes. She hadn't known why she'd had this effect on the woman. And she'd gone to her instinctively, had been pulled there so swiftly, she'd given no thought to repercussions. What effect her actions would have on the man who'd engaged her.

She'd discovered the answer to that quickly enough. She was, after all, still paying for this simple error. But the woman's effect on her was something she tried never to think about. But Reese had unearthed this, too. Carver had allowed that remark to escape, admitted she'd wanted a mother, thought she'd found one in Ingrid. She'd admitted these things to Reese. Things she'd staunchly refused to admit to herself. Things she'd always avoided, fully believing they'd take her to places far worse than any Santerre could devise.

Her hand brushed her knee. She found herself stroking a small scar through a hole in her jeans. A piece of glass from their floor had lodged permanently inside, forming a small blue-gray bump. She stroked it still as Tony turned into Santerre's driveway.

He was waiting for her. She made her way to the study as usual, though the sound of her flat shoes on the marble reminded her she wasn't dressed properly. But when she encountered him, she found that he, too, was dressed less formally—no jacket, no tie, his shirtsleeves rolled up. Instantly she regretted not taking the drug, forgetting the damn drug.

Then she saw it—the chain around his neck. Now, she could see only his necklace. It brought her full circle to the place, the night, she'd worked so hard to escape. He fingered the chain first, and then the vial suspended from it. She knew what the vial contained. That a piece of her flesh floated in the green-yellow liquid. His trophy, his proof that his men had done their job.

"I'm surprised you kept that," she said.

"No you're not," he answered.

As usual, he was right. Though ordinarily obscured, hidden beneath his shirt and tie, the necklace was always there.

She took her place on the couch, but he did not bring her a drink. She reached for her bag, retrieved the syringe, but he was coming toward her. Before she'd registered motion he was sitting beside her—he had the ability to move quickly without seeming to move at all. And he'd taken the implement from her easily enough, then he tossed it on the coffee table. She watched the syringe roll across the tabletop. She kept watching until it stopped, having hit the edge of a file folder.

"I have something for you," Santerre said. "Something you'll enjoy much more than that."

And before she realized it, he had her hair in his hand. He pulled at it, tipping her head back slightly. Then he'd slipped something into her mouth. She noticed a bitter taste as it began to dissolve, felt Santerre pulling at her hair. Then his other hand was at her throat, smoothing it as one would with a recalcitrant household pet.

He uttered soothing words or sounds as she felt the pill slipping down. And then she was following it, going under so fast, too fast. Her last conscious sensation was one of gagging, but she could not have said whether this was caused by the remnants of the pill or his well-placed hand.

Reese had finally arrived at home. Chilled and achy from her frantic walk, she went directly to the bathroom. She turned faucets, drew a bath, hoped this would calm her. She hadn't bothered to check her mailbox. Now, she ignored the flashing number on her answering machine. Instead she paced her apartment as she waited for the tub to fill.

When it had, she sank into the water determined it would soothe her. And against her expectations, it did. She found herself submerged, and then floating. Slowly she drifted, away from the present, until she found herself nearly nodding in the hot, scented water. Nodding nowhere, suspended.

Then, suddenly, without the present to hold her, she went from this sweet limbo to the only other available place—her past. And then she bolted, heaved herself up and out of the tub and was already standing before the sink, wrapped in her terry-cloth robe.

She ran cold water, splashed her face, forcing herself to stay aware and present through these actions. She made her way to bed, thinking again of Carver. And unable to shake these thoughts, she found herself right back where she'd started.

As she got into bed, Ingrid's words clouded her mind. The whole cryptic exchange between the woman and Carver lay before Reese once more. It swamped her, pulling her this way and that. She wrestled with all of it—who was playing who, who was winning. But most of all she fought the image of Carver in Santerre's bed.

. . .

That bed was where Carver awoke. She'd regained herself only to discover he'd captured her again. The thin, tight band encircling her neck was the first indication. Her arms ached, caught as they were behind her back. The crisp new leather of his belt cut into her wrists. And he'd removed her clothes.

Santerre sat on the edge of the bed. His pose resembled a concerned parent attending a child who's fallen ill. As her eyes flickered, he leaned closer. And, as he did this, the chain, the vial, dangled close. It swung back and forth, sending odd little shadows across her face.

He spoke then, his voice imitating the same concern as his pose. "Are you comfortable?"

Carver gave no answer to this, and so he continued.

"Ah, Nina, always so stubborn."

He slipped his hand into his pocket, extracted his penknife, and opened it. She lay perfectly still as he stroked her face with the blade—its flat surface, not its edge. And so he'd left it up to her—whether to move and cause the cut. Carver remained absolutely still.

"How is my wife?"

Again, Carver stayed mute.

In response Santerre traced her lips with the knife. He did this in a way that forced Carver to open her mouth—the only way to avoid being cut. And then the blade was on her tongue.

"Have you no need for this anymore?" Santerre asked, turning the blade ever so slightly. And while the question was plain and specific, it was larger, too.

Carver still said nothing at all. She held her tongue—held it as still as he held the blade.

"I can't understand you. All this time you refuse to see

her, and then you run to her? I indulge you. I abide by your requests. And what do I receive in return? Gratitude? Loyalty? No. You offer me deceit and betrayal. These are the ways you choose to repay my generosity?"

He turned the blade another fraction, applied a bit more pressure. Then he said, "Answer me."

Carver could taste it all—the acid metal, a hint of thick-sweet fluid, his satisfaction. These things combined, pooling like beads of tincture from a medicine dropper. And while she would not swallow it, she did absorb it. About this, he'd left her no choice.

Reese still lay awake. She'd given up trying to sleep, had let go of the tossing and turning. She preferred this, would rather let her mind keep churning than go to her dreams. But tonight, even though she stayed awake, she couldn't keep Frank away. She tried to push him aside, concentrate instead on Carver, on Ingrid and Santerre. But Frank kept coming at her. And when he did, she had to shake herself, actually shake her head—the only way to snap back into focus, because when Frank came everything blurred. Everything always blurred.

Tonight he was impossible to fend off. As usual, she blamed fatigue, working too hard, too long, not eating right. She blamed all the little things so she could continue to avoid the large ones.

Carver. Every time her mind went to Carver, Frank seemed to come along. The blurring would begin even before he arrived. Carver and Santerre. The two together losing shape, bleeding together until replaced—exchanged for the hulking, clouded image of Frank. First coming toward her, then lying there—bleeding into her carpet. The sodden mess she'd made of him. And, the other thing no one else knew: She'd waited.

Oh, she'd told herself she'd been stunned, in shock. She still told herself these things were true. They were and weren't. She'd certainly been unhinged, but not unable. Not exactly. She'd waited. She could remember the sensation of waiting. She couldn't help remembering it, despite how hard she tried. And this sensation, so mingled with fear, always felt worse than the satisfaction. That, at least, had come by surprise. The wait was deliberate, calculated—a decision.

She bolted from her bed again. This time she found herself in the kitchen, bottle in one hand, glass in the other. And once she'd poured the drink, her tight grasp on the glass reminded her of the way Carver'd held that syringe. And while she told herself what she'd told the girl, she was thinking its opposite, or a variant. She was thinking—this isn't working so get something stronger.

Santerre had released Carver. She'd dressed, collected her envelope. She was now back in the limo. There was no light to speak of so the only way to assess the damage was touch. She put one hand to a wrist, felt the burns and little cuts. She hesitated before doing the same with her neck, but forced herself. As soon as she touched her throat, she felt it closing, felt the gagging again—as if his hand was still around it, or his belt. She dropped her hand. But the sensation lingered, and her tongue was swollen, had pulped on either side of the slice. He was old-fashioned in this way—an eye for an eye.

She felt fear, too. She was still unaccustomed to this. Or, more accurately, she'd been so accustomed to it she'd rarely even noticed it; she'd never had to actually feel it. But she felt it more and more these days. It seemed like the only thing she did feel, and, for this, she blamed or credited Reese.

Without words, Santerre had made clear what her course of action ought now to be. Just who she should report back to. Carver didn't know if she would tell Reese any of it, whether she would even keep their appointment.

She recalled the detective's studied delineation of risk assessment. Carver would've laughed except for the soreness in her throat and mouth. She closed her eyes, but this only sharpened her image of Santerre—the one she couldn't shake. She still saw him, still saw the vial, dangling down as he'd engaged in his ritual. As he'd snorted the cocaine dumped from his other vial. With this image came thoughts of her vial—Blue Heaven—the one thing she owned and could count on.

When Tony dropped her off she went directly to it, recovered it from the desk, from the drawer. And now that she had it secured in her bag, she could go upstairs, could go to sleep, though it took another needle to achieve this. But sleep did come—an utterly black and dreamless sleep.

Sleep eventually came to Reese as well. And hers, too, artificially aided, remained free of dreams. The booze had accomplished this. She'd made herself drunk enough to blot it all. Reese had stumbled back to bed already out, gone, completely blotto.

THURSDAY

Twenty-two   The next morning, Reese woke to the insistent bleating of her alarm. It began faintly, a ringing in her ear, before crashing through, splitting both ears, and, yes, her head ached. She made coffee, first dropping the filters, then the canister. She would've laughed at herself, at her picture-perfect hangover, but she couldn't quite muster humor. She wasn't able because the amnesia the booze had created proved temporary.

It had all come crashing back, had crashed through just moments behind the alarm. Frank had, and Reese wasn't at all used to facing him during the day. But there he was. One minute she'd see him lying in her bed, waiting for coffee. Then the next minute she'd see him lying beside her bed, bleeding. For this new development, these daylight visions, Reese blamed or credited Carver.

She pulled herself together—showered, dressed, got herself out the door. And though she usually liked the walk to work, today she managed just two blocks up, made it only as far as Fifth Avenue and Thirteenth before hailing a cab.

As she dragged herself into the station house all the noise assaulted her. She trudged upstairs to the squad room, then to her desk. She felt as if she were groping for her chair. And then she sat down to face Miller.

"Rough night?" he asked her.

"What?" Reese asked, though she'd heard him. She just wasn't sure how far the question went.

"You look—"

"What?" she said, interrupting him. Her voice coming out sharp, hostile even.

"Tired, you look tired."

Reese pulled herself back. She reminded herself Miller didn't know, couldn't know how she spent so many of her nights. That he didn't have a dossier on her. No one here did. Well, except Harris. Harris had her file. But they all knew the story. Everyone knew the story. Everyone knew she'd killed Frank.

She shook her head as she had so many times the night before. She couldn't have Frank coming at her here.

"You sure you're okay?" Miller asked.

"I'm fine, it's you I'm worried about."

"Me? What about me?"

"Not here," she said, getting up.

Reese led Miller down to the garage. They sat in their car.

"So, you tired?" she said.

"What?"

"All your nights out there watching Carver. They getting to you? Or did someone already get to you? Have they had you right from the start?"

"What the hell are you saying?"

"I don't know, Gus. Best I can think is you're lying. Lying about going out there at all. Because otherwise you're lying about what you saw."

"I'm not lying about anything, and nobody got to me. And I'll tell you exactly what I saw yesterday."

"Yesterday?"

"Yeah. After I dropped her at Grand Central, I went out there. She'd acted so strange in the car. Didn't say a word, not a single word to anything I said. Like I wasn't even there. Like she wasn't even there. It spooked me, worried me. So I go out and I wait. Her car's there, no lights on. I'd made good time, but I'm wondering if somehow she beat me back. Then, later, a limo turns in her driveway, and she gets out. Hurries on inside. Limo leaves, then nothing. Rest of the night nothing."

"And the night before?"

"I told you, she stayed in."

"That's not what Carver told me. She said she was with Santerre."

"By the time I got there, everything was quiet. And I stayed until six in the morning. So either she'd got back already, or they brought her back after I left. Listen to me. You and me were both thinking if she moved, she'd take her car. Or we were looking for someone coming after her. I didn't know he was having her chauffeured around. Hell, even yesterday, I didn't know whose limo that was, not for sure. Least I'm telling you what I know. When'd you find out about her and Santerre?"

"Yesterday," she said, then paused. She was still evaluating both him and what he'd said.

"That's some neat trick," he said, then gave a low whistle.

The sound took Reese all the way back to viewing the body—reminded her how much she'd needed Miller's help to get through that. How he'd been the one who'd helped her stay grounded. The only one.

"How'd you get it out of her?" Miller asked now.

"Putting her with the wife," Reese said, coming back.

Back to trusting him. "There's something else we got. The wife owns a bunch of houses. Owns the one we staked out."

"She gave you that?"

"No, Eleanor dug it up."

"The wife owns them? What the hell does that mean?"

"I don't know yet. I'm going to put it in her face, see what happens. But for now, I need you to nose around." She rummaged her pocket, pulled out the list Eleanor'd given her. "Here's all of it: addresses, closing dates. I want you to see what the pattern is. See if there is one."

"Get the girls talking?"

"That's the idea."

"But wouldn't they hide it better than this?"

"Look, I don't know what they're playing. And I don't know who else is playing along. It's beginning to seem like one big setup to me. Us just caught in it, along for the ride. You getting me?"

"Uh-huh."

"But you'll do it?"

"Yes."

Reese felt her shoulders loosen, but her back stayed tight. "Look," she said, "I've got to get out of here. I'm meeting Carver. If I keep her waiting, she'll bolt for sure. If she even shows at all."

"I'll drive you down."

"No, I think I'd better cab it. How'd she look?"

"Huh?"

"Last night, how'd she look?"

"Couldn't tell much. But she sure seemed eager to get out of that car."

Without another word, Reese was gone.

Twenty-three   Reese breathed a little easier now, out in the open, on the street, but the sensation of relief didn't last long. Soon that familiar Manhattan feeling hit her—going out for air, only to discover there isn't any.

She hailed another cab, hoping she'd still get there early.

She told the driver to take her to Washington Square Park, and as she did she couldn't help but wonder what had prompted her to pick this meeting place—so far from the station house, so close to her apartment. And as she wondered this she couldn't quite pretend it had been for Carver's comfort. She knew it had been for her own. Though her apartment didn't seem very comfortable these days. It didn't seem safe anymore.

She'd taken the apartment when she still worked the Ninth. It had made sense then—close to but outside her precinct. She'd decided early on never to live in the precinct she worked. After the incident, after Frank, Eleanor had suggested she move. But Reese had dismissed the idea, citing all the practical reasons. Now she wished she'd listened.

She shook her head again, tried to focus on Carver. Reese could only hope she'd show. But when the cab dropped her on the curb, north of the park, she could see her—already there, waiting near the arch, though it was at least ten minutes before the time they'd set.

The last thing she needed was to startle Carver, so Reese approached her as calmly as she could: She tried not to hurry, and she made sure Carver could see her coming.

"Been waiting long?" she asked.

"Not really," Carver said. And, though her eyes still darted around, she seemed to relax a little. Reese kept her eyes on Carver. Mechanically, professionally, she noted the bruises and cuts on the girl's neck. She made no mention of them for the moment, nor did she mention Carver's early arrival. What she said was, "Come on, let's sit down."

She led Carver to an empty bench in an empty part of the park. Once they were sitting, Reese chose her words carefully. "I thought you didn't let him tie you anymore."

The words didn't leave much room for escape. Carver did pull at her shirt collar. She even buttoned it, though this clearly caused her discomfort. Soon she'd opened it again. All this fidgeting taking very little time, but seeming to go on forever.

"I don't," she said finally. "I didn't let him. He . . . he . . ."

Reese could see the fight going on inside the girl. She made her voice very gentle, very soft. "He what? What the hell did he do to you?"

"He knows. Okay? He knows everything."

"Tell me what he did."

"I shouldn't even be here."

"But you are here. Tell me."

Carver looked into Reese's eyes. Gave the detective a long stony look before she spoke, but she did begin to speak.

"He drugged me. I don't know what he used." Carver paused. She dropped her gaze. "I didn't see it coming. I don't know what it was. I didn't see it. The pill, I didn't see it.

He'd got it in my mouth before I even saw it. Of course, he can get his hands on anything." And with this she looked up again, but not at Reese. She looked past her when she said, "Sure got his hands on me."

Reese wanted to say something, anything, but there was nothing she could be sure would work, so she stayed quiet.

Carver looked down at her hands. There was an odd calm to the moment, and when Reese saw the cuts and burns on Carver's wrists, she reached her hand out and Carver took it.

"He did this to me then, once," Carver said. "Before, when I was with them both. I suppose he might've killed me that night. She thought so. I know she thought so. That's when I figured out about the daughter, when I finally asked her. I think she thought I knew. I suppose I did. I mean, I know it happens all the time, but it's still . . . You'd just rather think something else.

"So, I thought she was off in some boarding school. You know, Switzerland or something. I didn't know what I'd . . . who I'd gotten myself messed up with. I couldn't've, right? Could I?"

"No," Reese said.

"Last night was like back then, or sort of. He acted like he did back then. Like that night back then when he slipped me a pill and I woke up tied with his belt, and him going at me. But then I dropped off again. Next I know he's gone, and she's there. Cleaning me up, babying me.

"I ask her about the daughter. She tells me she found her same as me—tied up and turning blue. She doesn't say much more. She doesn't have to. She tells me I should leave. That he's gone for a while, and I should get out.

"I tell her she's the one should get out. I did this because I couldn't leave without her. I can't explain it, not in any way that makes sense to anyone. Doesn't make sense to me either, not really. You'd have to have seen her when I met her. How she was. You'd have to have felt what I felt for her, and I don't think anyone feels what I feel for her. Except maybe him, and where does that leave me?

"We were going to go together. It was her idea. I guess I let her down. I didn't believe she'd do it. And I knew it wouldn't work. Or at least I didn't think it would. So she left without me, left me alone in that house. Have you seen the house?"

Reese shook her head. She'd only driven by, seen only the gates.

"It's like . . . well it's big, like a compound or something. Like some kind of maze you can't fucking find your way out of. I couldn't, anyway. Not then. Do it all the time now, but not then. Not right away. I couldn't believe she'd done it. I waited three days there. Not sleeping, not eating, drinking some. Drinking maybe a lot. I waited for her to come back. I kept waiting for her to come back.

"Then it got eerie. The kind of quiet that worries you. I called a cab. Simple as that, I called a cab. And I'm thinking maybe it's done. After a while I'm thinking maybe it's really done. But like he knows just when I'd be thinking this, that's when he sends them. Has me cut.

"Couple, three days after that, his car comes to pick me up."

"You didn't call the police?"

Carver looked at Reese, looked her up and down. Then she said, "Who do you think cut me?"

"You tell me," Reese said.

"Couple of moonlighting cops on his payroll. That's how it works out there. Work so different down here?"

Reese certainly wasn't going to share her thoughts on that, but her face must've changed, shown something because Carver said, "I didn't think so."

Reese didn't acknowledge the remark. She steered the girl back, asked, "What happened then?"

"I went on his payroll. Can't beat 'em, join 'em. The house, the dope, the whole deal."

"And her?"

"He'd found her, of course. Had her found. At least he didn't find us together. At least I played that part right. And I acted cold on her, told him I wouldn't see her. He liked that. I could tell he liked that. At first he did, though it meant something was missing. Always missing.

"We made this arrangement. For years now we've kept this bargain, except it doesn't really work. It's never worked. Not for me, or him either. But we keep at it because . . . Well, I guess because of her. To get at her. Though I guess there's all kinds of ways to do that now. Don't need me for it."

"Did you know?"

"Know what?"

"About the girl he killed?"

"No."

"But you knew he went to the houses."

"Like I said, something was missing the way we worked it. He needs her. He needs her there. It's part of it for him."

"And you?"

"What?"

"You need her?"

Carver looked away. "I do my job."

"Then why you?"

"Huh?"

"Why you? Why you for so many years?"

"Simple. Fucking stupid simple. I look like her. The daughter, I mean. That's it. All it is—family resemblance. They made me one of the fucking family."

Reese didn't know what to say to this. She needed to tackle the present, but she wasn't quite done with the past. And she could see Carver might never be done with it.

"So what did he do last night?" she finally said.

"I told you already, he drugged me. And you can see how I woke up. Just like back then, tied and . . ." But here she stopped, and when she began speaking again, her voice had changed—had gone from impatient to hushed. She said, "He didn't fuck me. Least, I didn't wake up to that, him doing that. If he doesn't need me for that anymore . . . What the hell else is there?"

"What did he want?"

"Huh?" Carver said, fear in her voice, all across her face.

"When you woke up, what did he want from you?" Reese asked, trying to keep her own voice steady, her own fears contained.

"Information, or—that's not it. He asked about his wife. He said, 'How's my wife?' Something like that. But he didn't want to know. That wasn't the point. He just wanted me to know."

"Know what?"

"That he knows. Knows I saw her. Knows I've been talking to you. I told you already. He knows everything."

"But you didn't tell him anything?"

And Carver laughed, almost. It wasn't quite a laugh, more of a sneer. "No, I didn't tell on you. Didn't have to, did I? Besides, he had his knife in my mouth at the time. Made a little slice in my tongue. Nothing serious, really. The mouth heals fast. But still, all this talking, it's beginning to hurt."

Reese still had Carver's hand in hers, had kept hold of it this whole time, though it was something they'd both forgotten until now. Now the detective tightened her grip. "Look," she said, "this has gone far enough. Too far. You can't go back out there."

Carver's hand turned in Reese's.

Reese kept talking. "We can protect you. We can put you someplace safe."

"You don't believe that. If you did, would we be meeting here? Come on, Detective. You don't believe that any more than I do."

It was true. Reese didn't believe it. But she was determined—desperate to keep Carver from going back out there. And so it was in desperation that she offered her apartment. The words stumbled from her mouth. "My place," she said. "It's just a block or so up."

Carver looked incredulous. Reese felt disbelief herself. She certainly couldn't convince herself the girl would be safe there. Or that she'd stay. But Carver was going along with it. Both of them had already gotten up from the bench. Together they pressed ahead with this very questionable plan.

. . .

As Reese took Carver into her apartment, she felt ridiculous—telling her to make herself at home, offering her a drink.

Carver simply said, "Where's the bathroom?"

Reese showed her, understanding the question too well. Carver was already rummaging her bag, practically had the syringe in hand.

Reese waited it out. And when Carver'd returned, Reese made more lame comments, realizing she didn't want to leave. But she had to get back. Had to put those questions about the houses to Ingrid. She'd thought of asking what Carver knew about this, if she knew about it, but she didn't want to risk it, risk setting Carver off.

So Reese continued with small talk. "Well," she said, "I guess you can find what you need. There's some food, coffee. TV's in the bedroom."

Carver said, "Isn't that your friend's name?"

"What?"

"Your lawyer friend, isn't her name Coffee, something like that?"

"Yes, why?"

"I saw it on a file at Santerre's. Thought he was buying a plantation or something, except it was spelled funny."

Reese tried to act calm. She kept her voice steady as she said, "Huh," then added, "Well, anyway, I'd better be getting back."

Then Reese left. She left Carver in her apartment, unguarded. And in doing so, Reese left herself unguarded. Open to just about anything.

Twenty-four   Reese decided to walk back to the station house. She wanted time to think, to understand her own actions. She didn't like how they were adding up. That last thing Carver'd said had really thrown her. If Santerre had a file on Eleanor, it certainly wasn't the only file he had. Still, Carver hadn't exactly sounded sure about it. Reese couldn't quite believe it, just as she couldn't quite believe she'd put Carver at her place.

As Reese walked, she worked up a cover story. One to explain why it'd made sense to bring Carver into her home. But coming up with some story didn't make any sense. She would tell no one she'd done this. She was inventing stories to tell herself. Internal cover-ups.

If this was where time to think was taking her, then she didn't want to take the time. At Sixth Avenue and Twentieth—strung along by her own thoughts, strung up by them—she hailed a cab. And as her feet hit the sidewalk outside the station house, she felt some relief being back here. Could pretend for the moment that she was any other cop on any other case.

Reese went down to the basement, down to Ingrid's cell. She waved the guard away. She didn't want to go into the cell, hoped she could avoid this. Ingrid saw her. They faced each other through the bars.

Reese said, "Tell me why you own those houses. Why the titles are in your name."

Ingrid looked very tired. She spoke wearily, "Another clever trick of his. I asked him not to bring any more girls home. After Nina, I begged him not to. I couldn't stand it anymore, having that go on in our house. And he agreed to this. So instead he bought houses. First Nina's house. Then those other houses. He was always putting papers in front of me to sign, so I guess I signed those papers, too. Well, I know I did because he put them in my face. Told me he'd done as I asked. Given me what I asked for. That I asked for it.

"And despite this, to spite me, he continued to bring Nina into our home. Only Nina, because I'd asked him to stop after her. He'd caught me in my own words, turned them back on me. All these years she's refused to see me, while he's had her in my bed. And when he wanted others, wanted me, he'd take me to the most beautiful hotels and make them ugly. So much ugliness, so many years of ugliness."

Reese stayed quiet. Ingrid's hand rested on the bars, and Reese put her hand over it. She held her hand there a little while, and then, without a word, she left. Reese walked down that dingy alleyway. And reaching the foot of the stairs, she noticed the clock there, then checked her own watch. It was nearly five. More than six hours had passed. This seemed impossible to her.

Reese started climbing the stairs to the squad room. Halfway there, she heard Miller call out to her. She turned to see him bounding up after her. She met him halfway. He huddled her into the corner of a landing, then said, "Bingo."

"What?" she said. "What'd you get?"

"Not here," he said.

He hauled her down the stairs, back out on the sidewalk. "What'd you get?" she asked again.

"Not here, either," he said. "Let's go to your place."

Reese laughed aloud. Miller was already hailing a cab. Apparently he, too, had decided against using the company car today. He gave the driver the address, and she didn't stop him. As they rode the elevator to her floor, she became nearly punchy. Maybe he could guard Carver. Maybe they could talk in the laundry room. Maybe she was losing it.

"Hey," he said as she simply turned the knob and walked in. "Cops not even locking up. What're you, nuts?"

She didn't answer him. And she didn't bother to lock the door behind them. "You want a drink?" she asked.

"Sure, why not. On duty, off duty, it's all turning into the same thing."

She poured the drinks, carried them over to the coffee table. Miller was already waiting on the couch, but before she sat down with him, she glanced into the bedroom. She wasn't looking for Carver, she was looking to see if Carver had nosed around. She couldn't actually tell. She saw the marble brick on her bedside table—bagged as evidence, and then returned to her after that perfunctory IAB investigation. And she'd kept it. She'd put it right back where it belonged. As she looked at it she wondered if Carver had noticed it.

She shut the bedroom door. She knew Carver probably hadn't even taken the time to poke around. She'd probably been out the door right behind Reese. But then she'd known this would happen.

She sat down with Miller, tried to push Carver from her mind and focus on him. "So what'd you get?" she said.

"Two talkers. Two different houses. Same story. Same as that one you talked to. Cherise."

"And?" Reese said.

"Looks like it works this way: Santerre buys a house, or his wife does . . ."

"No, I talked to her. Just another sick joke of his, putting the titles in her name."

"Nice. Anyway, Santerre buys the house, has it stocked, plays till he kills, then moves on."

"So he buys the places first?"

"These girls aren't exactly precise about time. You know, they'll say spring a few years ago, something like that. But you pin 'em down a little and that's how it figures. How it fits with those dates you gave me on the closings."

"So both these girls started after Santerre owned the houses?"

"One did. The other one's older." Miller fished in his pockets, pulled out his notebook, flipped the pages. "Here's how she puts it: 'We get new management, then they start bringing in all this new blood, fresh ones, young ones. I start getting my shifts cut.' Then there's a lot of blah, blah, blah about chargebacks, what a bundle she made before the new management, stuff like that. Oh, and how the young ones get treated when they go with, get this, 'the Voodoo King.' That's what she called him.

"So, finally I steer her back. She's talking about all this like it's over. So I asked her when it stopped, and she says,

'When he found a keeper.' You like that one? They all think these girls go on to greener pastures."

"What'd she say happened then?"

"Management went back from hands-on to hands-off. Though I got another earful about chargebacks. Guess that part didn't change."

"The other girls?"

"Huh?"

"The ones who went with him. They still there?"

"Nope. Quit. She was pretty bitchy about them."

"And the young one?"

"Same story, different angle. Recruited from Spence— you know that high-tone high school. Didn't know what the hell she was in for, I could tell that."

"How old?"

"Claims she's twenty-one now, of course. But the numbers don't add. Guess those private schools aren't much on math. I'd put her at fifteen, sixteen at most."

"And she's still working?"

"Yep. Took to it, apparently. Probably had some training at home."

"So how's she tell it."

"Well, she's a piece of work. Talks money, money, money. Not going to wind up like her mother, shit like that."

"Like what?"

"Not going to get tied down for the cash, to one man. Marry rich is what she's been told, and doesn't like being told. She calls Santerre Voodoo Man. Says she'd get called in when he came. Could tell he was the overlord—her word. Opposite of your one, she didn't want to go with him. Would hang back.

"She did talk to some of them who went and came back.

Said the same as yours. Narced out, pampered. But she said something else, too. Said they'd been knocked around. Noticed bruises on their wrists and neck."

Hearing this, Reese picked up her drink. She'd fucked up. Her stupid play with Carver meant she hadn't set up another meeting with her.

"Hey," Miller said. "You getting this?"

"Yeah, yeah. Making me a little sick is all. Can we fast-forward?"

"Not much else, really. But we've got our pattern."

"Don't suppose either of them will talk for real."

"Not likely."

"So now he's a fucking game warden," Reese said, putting down her drink just as Miller picked up his again.

"That's what it looks like," he said.

"That young one, she say anything about the wife? Anything at all?"

"Nope."

"And the other one didn't?"

"Nope," Miller said. He leaned back on the couch, sipped his drink. Reese was reaching for hers again when he said, "Wait a minute." He'd put down his drink. Flipped through his notebook again. "Wait, wait. Here it is. Not much, but the young one says—she's talking about avoiding him, hanging back and all. She says, 'I'm not stupid.' Man, they all say that, don't they? Like we are?"

"Gus . . ."

"Look, it's not much, but she says, 'I'm not stupid. I'm not going to get roped by this asshole. Already got a fucking mother and father. Sure don't need another set.' "

"You didn't ask her? You didn't follow it?"

"Went right by me. I'll go back, okay? Tomorrow, first thing. I'll find her again. I know how to find her."

Reese slowed herself down. She couldn't exactly dress him down for this. Not when her own blunder lay so starkly before her. "Yeah, okay. Look, you got a lot. Lot more than I thought you would. Just not sure what we do with it."

"We could start crossing dates with missing persons, or Jane Doe bodies."

"Don't have time. Even if we did it'd be too shaky. Besides, we'd need help. It'd tip them off."

Miller put his notebook on the table, and they sat quietly for a while. Reese could feel him wanting to ask about her meeting with Carver, could feel him holding off.

"You tell Harris any of that?" Reese asked, gesturing to his notebook.

"No. Should I've?"

"No."

More quiet before Reese asked, "You think we should be telling him anything?"

"I don't think so, not anymore."

"Santerre knows about Carver. That we've been talking to her. Using her's more like it."

"Yeah?" Miller said. Then Reese could hear him trying to sound casual when he asked, "So how'd that go with her today? She show?"

"Yep. With belt burns on her neck and wrists."

Miller gave his low whistle. Again the sound took Reese back to when they'd viewed the body together. From here she asked, "They ever ID her?"

"Who?" he asked. Then sheepishly, catching himself, he said, "Truth is, I don't know."

"You think we're playing their game after all? Following all these dirt roads to nowhere?"

"What? You got nothing from her?"

"I got plenty. You got plenty. But we still don't have anything we can stick to him."

"But what'd you get?"

Reese recounted her conversation with Carver, and as she neared the end, she weighed telling him about bringing her here. And because they were here, because Miller was in her apartment—the place she'd killed her last partner— she wanted to ask him what he knew about that. Which version of the incident he'd heard. Which one he believed.

Incident. What a clean, misleading word. Reese remembered how she'd reacted when Ingrid had used the word accident to describe her daughter's murder. How disgusted she'd been as the woman insistently clung to that word. How crazy it felt to utter it herself in order to elicit the desired response. Accident. Incident. What was the fucking difference?

She'd drifted off, stopped midsentence apparently, because Miller said, "You going to finish?"

"That's pretty much it," she said. She left out the part about bringing Carver home. And she certainly wasn't going to ask him any of those other questions.

"You think he's going to kill her," Miller said, and it wasn't a question.

"What?" she said, stalling again, afraid of what was showing on her face, what he could hear in her voice.

"It's what you're thinking, isn't it? What anyone would be thinking? He starts in on old tricks . . ."

"Funny."

"I didn't mean that. You know what I meant. He starts stringing her up again, drugging her. Hasn't in years. How else you add that?"

But Reese didn't answer.

Miller said, "Where is she anyway?"

"Huh?"

"Carver. Where is she?"

"Home by now, I guess."

"So, I'll go back out there . . ."

"No, wait a minute. There's something she said. You talk to Eleanor today?"

"No, not today."

"I got to call her."

"Why, what is it?"

"Just wait a minute."

Reese looked around for her cordless, brought it back to the couch. Then she tried every number—office, car phone, cell phone, home. They all came up empty, but the last one troubled her most. The machine didn't pick up, just endless ringing. She'd clicked off her own phone, but still held it in her hand.

"What's worrying you?" Miller asked.

"It's something Carver said. Said she saw a file at Santerre's with Eleanor's name on it. I mean, she didn't sound so sure about it. I didn't make much of it. But now Eleanor's not answering."

"And you think . . ."

"I don't know what to think. I've just got a bad feeling."

"So let's check it out."

"Yeah, yeah . . ."

They were both moving for the door. Out on the sidewalk,

it was pitch black save for streetlights and headlights. Reese checked her watch. Again hours seemed to have disappeared. It was nearly ten.

Miller glanced at his watch, too. "Late," he said. "Guess we go to her apartment."

"No, you check her office. I'll take the apartment."

"You sure we should split up?"

"Don't see another way. You know where it is, right?"

He nodded. Then they both hailed cabs.

Twenty-five   Carver had left Reese's place almost immediately, but she hadn't gone home right away. Instead she'd wandered the streets until her feet had begun aching. Then she'd ridden the subway, afraid otherwise she might return to the detective's apartment. She'd wanted to stay, had wished she could believe it'd be safe there, but that went way beyond stupid. She had to stay on the game—the one she knew how to play.

Finally she'd landed in Grand Central, but then she'd walked outside and hailed a cab. She wasn't going to get on some train and just sit through the ride. Not when she knew exactly who'd be out there, waiting to meet her. So instead she now sat in a cab, was taking this ride instead, and spending every minute of it with her hand clutching that vial of Blue Heaven—her last-chance escape.

Reese spent her cab ride with her hand on her gun. The uptown traffic was heavy, even at this hour. She wanted behind the wheel, kept urging on the cabbie, was cursing the other drivers before he did. And she cursed herself for being in a cab instead of a police car. Finally they'd hit Park between Ninety-forth and -fifth, were stopped at a light.

"This is good enough," Reese said, tossing money as she

opened the door. Soon as she hit the pavement, the light turned against her. She ran the avenue, weaving and dodging up and across it. A fucking Cadillac clipped her just as she made the curb, sent her skidding across the sidewalk. She righted herself, and kept running, sprinted the long crosstown block, while the Caddy's elderly driver screamed obscenities after her.

She rounded the corner, and darted into Eleanor's building. "She in?" she asked the doorman, slowing her pace as she passed him.

"Yes," he said.

She heard him, though she was already in the elevator, the doors already closing. As the elevator climbed, Reese already had her keys in hand, had picked Eleanor's out from the others. She had her gun out, too, had it tucked into her belt. The elevator opened. Reese stepped into the foyer, listened at the door, but heard nothing. Absolutely nothing.

She slipped the key into the lock and turned it, quietly opened the door, then slipped the keys back into her pocket. Drew her gun from her belt.

The apartment was completely dark. Reese walked it from memory. Was headed for the bedroom when she bumped something hard. Reese knelt down, felt the heavy coffee table, now lying on its side. Reese felt the carpet around it—soggy but not sticky. Her hand brushed the smooth glass of a bottle—it, too, on its side, more liquor spilling out when she jostled it.

Reese moved on. Her eyes had adjusted some. She could discern objects. She could see the bedroom door—a door she knew had a slight warp that kept it from ever fully closing. She paused again to listen. Still hearing nothing, she drew herself back, and gave that door one blistering kick.

First a dull thud, then scrambling. She scanned quickly, made out two hulking shapes. One on its knees, near her. The other on the bed. The near one lunged. He'd got his arms around her knees, was taking her down.

The cab had dropped Carver at her door. She'd gone into the house and up the stairs. No pause, no thought of anything else, she headed for the bathroom, for the bathtub. The lights in there were the only ones she bothered to turn on, and she did so only after she'd started the water running. And she kept them on just long enough to find and light a candle.

As the tub filled she shucked her clothes. Then she added oil to the water. She did this without any recollection of Ingrid. It wasn't until Carver eased herself into the tub, until she submerged her wrists and dipped her neck, that the stinging began. And once it had, the sensation immobilized her. Several minutes passed before she could clear her head, think to get herself up and out of the water.

She stood now beside the tub, water everywhere from her hurried exit. Even the candle doused by it. So there she was, shivering and groping in the dark. Tripping through her discarded clothes. As she found and put on her robe, her foot brushed her bag. She wanted to want it—the syringe inside. Even more, she wanted to want the vial—her vial. But she simply didn't. All she really wanted was sleep. Genuine sleep. Not the synthetic imitation she was used to, but the real thing.

Still in the dark, she made her way to the bedroom. She dropped her robe on the floor beside the bed, then slipped between the well-worn sheets. But she still felt as if she were underneath water, with her throat and wrists burning, still burning. Finding herself stung and stunned, Carver could no longer escape Ingrid, couldn't fend her off anymore. The woman kept pulling her under and back. Back to the night Carver'd recounted to Reese. Ingrid had drawn her a bath that night, had roused her with cold water. Carver remembered coming to, thrashing about. Water everywhere. Stinging cold everywhere, and burning, too. These same spots burning.

Now, she could almost smell burning—a faint tinge of sulfur seeming to come before the sound, before the match strike. Then an ember, glowing from the far-corner chair. And though it seemed a shock, truly she'd been waiting for it, waiting for him. Carver'd been waiting for Santerre in the one part of her that remained permanently coiled.

Gus Miller had persuaded a security guard to take him up to Eleanor Coffey's office. He hadn't had to show his shield. He hadn't even had to say he was a cop. The guy just accepted his story about needing to pick something up after hours. Now as they got off the elevator and headed down the hall, the guard said, "You lawyers. Always busy, always working, always in a hurry. You work with those other ones? They in such a hurry they forget what they came for? Send you back for it?"

"Yeah," Miller said. "You know how it is."

"Sure do."

They'd reached the door. The guard unlocked it. He said, "Just make sure you lock it behind you." And then he'd left. Left Miller alone in the office to find neatly jimmied locks on each and every file-cabinet drawer. He sat down at the desk; the one locked drawer there, too, had been forced, though not as cleanly. He ran his fingers along splintered wood, then picked up the phone. He tried Eleanor Coffey's home number, but it just rang and rang.

Miller left the office, left the building, trying to think of the quickest way uptown.

Reese felt her knees buckling in his grasp. She palmed her gun, held tight to it, then slammed. The heavy hit cut his head. She felt the stickiness. Saw him tumble over, saw the other one coming at her. She had her gun on him, but he kept coming. She aimed low and fired. He kept coming, but slower, tilting, then pitching sideways. He began to drop.

Reese circled them. Turned. Put herself between the two of them and the bed. She looked back quickly, said, "Ellie?"

She got no response. She could see Eleanor on the bed, but not moving, not moving at all.

Reese looked at the men. The one she'd shot had roused the other one. They moved, staggering but fast—fast and out. The were getting gone. Would be gone if she didn't stop them. And she didn't. She let them go, while she went to Eleanor.

"You've been out again," Santerre said, his voice following the smoke from his cigarette.

Carver gave no answer, and so he said, "You do understand that I'd prefer not to hurt you."

Carver nodded, but made no audible sound.

Santerre continued, "But you also know I will do what is necessary."

"What do you want from me?" Carver asked, the words coming from her in something like a moan.

"I want your understanding."

Through half-open eyes Carver saw the ember coming toward her. And then she felt his weight on the bed.

"We do understand each other, don't we? Haven't we always? Always understood each other, and understood my wife. And so I expect you to understand what I tell you, now. What I've come here to tell you about her."

And Carver was nodding again, and she continued to nod as he continued to speak.

Reese felt for Eleanor's pulse. It was faint, faint but there. She felt for the phone. Found it, but it was dead. She needed light. Ran to the kitchen, to the circuit breakers, tripped all of them. Various lights flickered on in different rooms. She ran back to the bedroom. Turned the lights on in there. The phone'd come back, too. It was ringing. She grabbed it, said, "Yeah."

It was Miller. Thank God it was Miller.

"Call EMS," she told him. "And get here fast."

She turned back to Eleanor. She knew that look. She'd seen it enough times as a narc. Eleanor looked heavily drugged. She remembered what Carver'd said about Santerre feeding her that pill. Reese started shaking Eleanor, trying to rouse her, then hoisting her, walking her. And Eleanor groggily began coming around.

Then Miller was there, standing in the doorway. "She all right?" he asked.

"Yeah, help me walk her."

"EMS is on the way."

"You tell them you're a cop?"

"No."

"Good. Let's tell them our friend here just had a little too much to drink. Let them check her out. Then get them gone."

"There's blood everywhere."

Reese looked around. "Well, let's take her out to the living room."

Miller righted the coffee table, while Reese kept Eleanor walking. It didn't look too bad in here. A trail of blood led back to the service elevator, but Reese didn't think they'd spot it.

"How'd you get here so fast?" she asked Miller now.

"I was in the lobby. Doorman wouldn't let me up. Said no one was answering the intercom. They should have that guy working security down at her office. Down there, seems just about anyone can get in."

Reese listened about the broken locks, while she looked around the room. If they'd been after files, she'd guessed they'd found them here. From the looks of it Eleanor'd been on the couch working when they'd come in. Reese just now noticed her friend's fountain pen leaking ink into the carpet, near where that bottle still lay leaking booze. "Hey, Gus, would you pick that stuff up for me."

"Sure," he said. He put the bottle on the table, and the pen beside it.

"What's taking so long?" Reese said. "This neighborhood you'd think they'd be here by now."

"Maybe the doorman won't let them up either."

"Well, someone let in Santerre's thugs."

"Yeah, so what happened?"

She'd told him most of it by the time the paramedics arrived. Reese and Miller waltzed through that part pretty smooth. Eleanor'd begun talking, though fuzzily. The paramedics checked her over, then gave the usual drill—admonitions about mixing liquor with prescription medication—then left.

Once they'd gone, as soon as they'd gone, Eleanor let on that she was fully and sharply awake. But all she could remember was a struggle on the couch. Two men in navy coveralls, trying to get a pill down her throat. And, yes, she'd been working—going through her files on INISCO and the Santerres. And, yes, now all those files were gone.

Carver listened as Santerre finished his story. And as she finished it, she watched him begin unfastening his belt. Now, she wanted her vial—wanted to finish this herself. She wanted anything but to have him finish it for her.

Twenty-six   By the time Reese and Miller left Eleanor Coffey's apartment, Fifth Avenue was already crowded with morning traffic. "Shit," Reese said, as they got into the cab the doorman had waiting for them.

"If he's already started cleaning up . . . ," Miller began.

"You think he's done her already?"

"It doesn't look real good. Him trying something that bald-faced with Eleanor. Something he knows we'd find out in a minute . . ."

"But why now?" Reese asked.

"Maybe he knows something we don't."

The cab had crossed Central Park by now. As the driver waited to make the downtown turn, Reese was tempted to tell him to hit the highway instead, take them out to Carver's house or Santerre's. But she knew she and Miller had to go to their own house—the station house.

They pushed through the squad-room doors together. "You want coffee?" Reese said.

"Yeah, a couple of gallons ought to do it," Miller said. He sat down, absently opening a file that'd been left on his desk. But when Reese brought the coffee over, he grabbed her arm, said, "Get a load of this."

"What am I looking for?" she asked, picking up the file.

"Look under *cause of death*."

Reese did as he said. And as she did, she felt adrenaline taking hold, taking over, and then she exploded. "She fucking drowned? Takes four fucking days to find out she drowned."

She saw Harris watching her. Report in hand, she went straight for him, crashed into his office.

"How long you known about this? Huh? What else you got coming for me?"

"Detective . . ."

"What else?"

"Detective, sit down."

Harris closed the door and pulled the blinds.

"Detective, I said, sit down."

"You tell me what else you got coming to blindside me."

"I think you better stop right there."

"Oh, is that what you think?"

"That, and that you're not thinking at all."

"Yeah and you've got it all figured—"

"Reese, another word and you're off this case."

"You'd love that, wouldn't you?"

"Reese, shut up and listen. I told you what this was going to be, and you wanted it. Remember that? And I got that damn report this morning, same as you. Only reason I saw it first is you just waltzed in here.

"I don't know what to make of you lately, Detective. And I don't know what to make of that paper in your hand because you haven't been talking to me. You been going off like the Lone Ranger. You been going off down in the cells. You been going off in my squad room. And I've let you. I'll give you that, I've let you. Now, you want to make me regret that? Regret trusting you?"

He'd hit all the right nerves. This last one especially, a master stroke. Him talking about trusting her, when she sure as hell didn't trust him. He hadn't gotten to her this time, but he had slowed her down. She wasn't yelling anymore when she said, "Do we know when Santerre got it?"

"I assume his lawyer received it this morning, just like everyone else."

Reese held her tongue, but just barely.

"So you tell me, Detective, what do we make of this?"

"I don't know yet. I need to get with the wife." But already Reese had pictured the daughter, remembered Ingrid saying she'd put her in a bathtub. "She doesn't know yet, right?"

"We save her for you."

Reese started for the door, but Harris held his hand up, stopped her.

"Do it up here, Reese. And use interview three."

"Oh, you want three, do you? Why's that? So you can screw . . ."

"No, so you can use what you get."

"And you can get over . . ."

"You know better."

"Do I?"

"You better know. I told you from the start to play by the book, and you've done everything but. And I've done nothing but give you slack. Now I'm reeling some in because I give you any more, you're going to hang yourself. We understand each other?"

"Completely."

"Good. Go on, now, Detective. Do your job."

Reese left Harris's office, and crossed the too-quiet squad room. She went to her desk and called down for Ingrid. And she knew she had to call Eleanor. After the night they'd just been through, the last thing Reese wanted was to have to drag her friend in here. But she made the call, and Eleanor said she'd be right there.

As she waited for the guards to bring Ingrid, Reese could feel the other detectives looking at her while they pretended to look at paper. Now she did the same, glancing down at the report, while really she scanned the room.

"You want me in there with you?" Miller asked quietly.

"No. Thanks, but she won't talk with you there."

"You know something, don't you?"

"Nothing I can be sure about."

The squad doors opened. Everyone in the room watched as Ingrid was brought in. Everyone but Reese, who looked back to Harris's office. Watched him watching Ingrid through his now open blinds. Then his eyes met her own. He gave a slight nod. She nodded back. Then she turned to the guards—there were two, one on either side of the dazed woman—and said, "Put her in three."

They did what she said, did what they were told. It wasn't a hard job if you knew how to take orders.

Reese waited it out a bit. She wanted Ingrid nervous. But she didn't wait too long. They were all looking at her again, the other detectives.

So with the report in her hand, she went for the room. Once inside, she dismissed the guards. Now it was just Reese, Ingrid, and the autopsy report. Though outside, she knew they all watched. Through that damn two-way glass, she knew the whole squad was watching and listening.

"Have a seat, Mrs. Santerre," Reese said, opening simply.

But Ingrid backed away. She kept backing away from Reese until she bumped into a chair. Only then did she sit down at the table. But, once seated, she switched. Her face went from bewildered to stony. And her voice was chiseled precision when she said, "Well, what is it, Detective?"

Reese simply put the open folder down in front of her.

"I don't see. What is it you want me to see?"

"Look under *cause of death*, Mrs. Santerre. Read it. Read it to me."

"Why don't you tell me what it is you want?"

"I just did. Read it."

But the words blurred before Ingrid's eyes. Seemed to move around on the page. "I can't see it."

"No, you won't see it. Isn't that more like it, Mrs. Santerre?"

"Don't call me that. Please don't . . ."

"It's your name, lady."

"My name . . . Ingrid's my name."

"And your daughter's name again. What was it?"

Ingrid had slumped forward, but this only brought her closer to the word on the paper. She closed her eyes but she could still see it.

"Lila, wasn't that it? You kill her, too?"

"No, no. What are you saying?"

"Look at the paper."

"No." Ingrid sprang up, made it halfway to the door before Reese blocked her. They nearly collided, but Ingrid veered, kept veering away from Reese, from Reese's words.

"I think your husband's the one telling the truth. He's been covering for you all these years. Hasn't he?"

"No, you don't understand."

"I understand you're a liar."

"I didn't kill anyone."

"No? Then explain it to me."

Ingrid had wedged herself between the wall and a file cabinet. And Reese kept coming at her. Ingrid tried to turn away, but there was no room to move. Then she closed her eyes.

"Look at me," Reese yelled. "Look at me."

The woman's eyes snapped open. Her arm covered her head, protecting from the blow that still didn't come.

Reese kept pressing. "Come on, how'd it happen? Where'd the water come from?"

"I wanted to help her. I only wanted to help her."

"How, Ingrid? How?"

"He'd left. I drew a bath for her. I only wanted to get her loose, untie her. I thought . . ." Here she began to drift.

"What? What did you think?"

"That the water would help. Help me get her loose. Help rouse her. I thought I could make it all right. That it'd be all right if I could just get her loose. Get her to wake up.

"I carried her to the tub. She was so light. It wasn't like . . ." Ingrid began drifting again.

"It wasn't like what?" Reese asked, her voice gentler now, her hand reaching out.

"With . . ."

Reese took the woman's hand. Took it away from her face.

"With my daughter. The others. This one was so light. I

thought it'd come out different because she . . . because I could carry her. You see, don't you?"

Reese nodded, though she didn't see at all. She only saw tears—slow, quiet tears running down Ingrid's face.

"I put her into the tub. I tried to undo the knot. But the water made it worse. Everything was so slippery. I couldn't get to the knot . . ."

"What did you do? Ingrid, tell me what you did."

"I turned her, to get to the knot. She wasn't moving. She wasn't moving at all. Only when I moved her. And that went wrong. It all got turned around. Her face went into the water. I couldn't undo the knot. I couldn't move quickly enough. And she wasn't waking up. She wouldn't wake up. It all got so turned around. I wanted her to be all right. Like with Nina. Nina's all right."

Reese stiffened slightly.

"She is, isn't she? Still all right?"

"Yes, yes. She's fine." Though, of course, Reese couldn't be sure of this—feared its opposite and hoped her fear didn't show. "Where was your husband?" Reese asked now.

"He'd left her for dead. Gone to buy that hideous bag."

"And you?"

"I told you. I wanted to help her. I was trying to help her."

"Is that how you helped Lila?"

"What?"

"Did your daughter drown?"

Ingrid had thoroughly cornered herself. The only way out was through Reese. The woman couldn't even turn away, though she tried. Reese kept hold of Ingrid's hand, wouldn't let it out of her grasp. And when the woman closed her eyes,

Reese said, "Look at me, Ingrid. Ingrid, look at me. Did your daughter drown?"

The woman's eyes snapped open again. And in those eyes Reese saw only terror—crazed terror.

"Did she? While you were helping her, trying to help her? Is that what happened? Ingrid, look at me."

"No. No. Not what you're saying. It's not what you're saying."

"Tell me."

"He came in. She was alive. I'd gotten her awake with the water. I thought he'd come to help me. I asked him to help me. She was so heavy and I'm not a strong person. I couldn't lift her, not by myself. I couldn't get her out.

"He knelt beside me. I thought he'd come to help but . . ."

"Ingrid. Ingrid, what did he do?"

"He held her . . . He held her down. I tried to stop him. I'm not strong. I couldn't stop him. She was thrashing about. The water went everywhere. He pushed her head under the water. He held her head under the water. She was thrashing about. I pulled at his arm. He looked calm. He looked so calm.

"I pulled at his arm, and he hit me, and my head hit something else . . ."

"Ingrid. Ingrid, listen to me. Is that how it was at the hotel? Did he come in while you were helping her?"

"What?"

"The girl . . . Did your husband . . . Did he come in while you were helping the girl? At the hotel, Ingrid? Did he come in?"

"No . . . I was all alone. I couldn't make it right. I was trying to make it right. Her, she . . . I couldn't undo the knot. I couldn't turn her. She hadn't been heavy before. I thought I could get her out before he came back. I thought she'd wake up. Like Lila, like Nina. I thought I could get her to wake up. That then she'd be all right. That I could get her out before he came back and she'd be all right. But she wouldn't wake up. Nothing's all right. Except Nina. Nina's all right."

Reese looked ever-so-slightly away.

"She is, isn't she? You said she was."

"She's fine, Ingrid. She's all right." But all Reese could think was: get out there, get out there and make sure of it because too much time had passed. More than enough time had passed.

A knock on the door startled them both. They were both shaking now. Reese pulled herself away from Ingrid. Tried to pull herself together.

"Ingrid, go and sit down."

The woman simply obeyed while Reese went to the door.

It was Eleanor. She said, "Caroline, what is it? What's happened?"

Reese went to the table, retrieved the report, pointed to the applicable line.

"What the hell does this mean?"

"She did it," Reese said quietly, nodding toward Ingrid. "She did it after all. She admits it."

"What? How?"

"None of that matters. Look, stay with her. Don't let her alone. Don't let anyone at her. I've got to talk to Harris."

"Caroline, wait. Don't. He can't help you, now. He won't help you now."

"I know that."

Twenty-seven   When Burns arrived, Santerre was in his study, on the phone. He finished his call while Burns waited awkwardly.

As he put down the receiver, he said, "Seems my wife's down there confessing."

"Sir?"

"You did get the coroner's report? I sent it over last night. Hope I didn't wake you."

Burns could hear the edge in this last remark. Heard it working its way to the surface, through the surface of his client's apparent good mood. "Yes," Burns stammered, "but . . ."

"But what, Tom? I'd say it's just about finished. Despite last night's debacle. Those idiots."

"They did obtain the files, didn't they? They confirmed with me."

"Oh, yes. Have a look for yourself. The sodden mess is right there on the table. Given the look of them and what's inside, we may need to do a little extra cleanup work."

Burns glanced down at a stack of files slathered with blood. Then asked, "What was damaged?"

"Our two, not the lawyer. Seems her detective friend paid an unexpected visit. Disrupted things somewhat. But she's paying us back today. Securing my wife's confession."

"I don't quite follow you."

"Where's your confusion, Burns? Maybe you should seek other employment if you can't understand something so plain."

"Mr. Santerre, I didn't mean to suggest—"

"Don't start, Tom. It's a bit late for that. Get your hands a little too dirty on this one? That it?"

"No. Mr. Santerre, I only meant to say—"

"What? What is it you meant to say? Come on, Tom. Do you think I can't see that your feelings for me are, let's say, somewhat conflicted? Oh, don't look so nervous. I don't pay you to like me. And the money's nice. You like the money. Keeps that wife of yours happy. Keeps that daughter of yours in her fancy school. What was your daughter's name, Tom? Pretty girl, as I remember. But, then, I don't get to see her much.

"Remember my daughter, Tom? Remember Lila? Now, there was a true beauty. Terrible tragedy, my daughter's death, wouldn't you agree?"

Burns nodded.

"But we got through it. You were a great help, as I remember. I'd hate to think you'd outlived your usefulness. Terrible feeling, that one. So, where were we, Tom?"

But during this exchange Burns had lost the ability to speak.

"Oh, yes, I remember. My wife's confession. Why don't you go on down there, Tom. Keep an eye on things for me. I have a loose end of my own to tie up. When I've dispensed with it, I'll call for you. Then we'll put our heads together. See how best to care for my wife."

. . .

Carver woke shaky and grogged. Her nerves came alive one by one, made vivid pathways through an overall haze. He'd been coming at her with the belt, this much she remembered. Then a chirping sound had startled them both. He'd pulled something from his pocket, then he'd begun yelling. She'd thought he was yelling at her, but the words didn't fit. Then she'd realized he was on the phone, screaming, "You idiots. I give you a simple task and you . . ."

Then he'd thrown the phone. The small plastic gadget breaking to pieces as it hit the wall. He'd come at her again but the belt was gone. Instead he'd forced another pill down her throat. This one took her down so fast and heavy she was sure it was for keeps, had put her down for good. But all these hours later, here she was alive again, fighting her way out from under.

She forced herself out of bed. As she crossed the room, her foot hit a sharp bit of plastic—a remnant from his shattered phone. She made her way back to the bathroom. Put herself under cold water. A quick shower. No more baths, not today, maybe not ever, not after what he'd told her about Ingrid. And she had understood, she had believed what he'd said about Ingrid drowning that girl. She could see how it had happened. She knew just how it had happened. She knew all too well. "So, you see," he'd said, "my wife is guilty. And your detective friend will secure her confession. She will take care of my wife, just as I will take care of you."

So Carver understood she was alive simply because of a phone call. Only because a phone call had interrupted Santerre's plans, had required his immediate attention. And she believed, too, that Reese now had what she wanted. The detective had solved her case, and so would have no further use for her.

Carver wrapped herself in her robe. Her foot brushed against her bag, still lying there on the bathroom floor. She picked it up. Carried it with her back to bed. She rummaged right past the syringe to the vial. Her vial. She lay back, drifting again as her body went slack, slack, save for one hand—the one tightly clenching her vial.

Reese went back into Harris's office. He was on the phone, hung up as she slammed the door.

"I thought you'd've watched it," she said.

"I did."

"Look, he still did the daughter, and Gus found two working girls . . . he's done a string of hookers. I know he has. We can tie him to two."

"How?"

"We just need more time . . ."

"His lawyer's already on his way down here."

"That who you were talking to? What, you give them news updates?"

"They called me. I don't have to explain my . . . Don't go turning this around on me. Maybe if you'd told me some of this sooner we could've worked with it, but you've done this to yourself. You either give me something solid right now or it's over."

"She told me about the daughter. You listen to that part? Or you too eager to get on the phone? We exhume the body, or at least unearth the autopsy."

"Cremated before autopsy."

"Oh, I see. The news travels both ways."

"Reese, I've had about enough . . ."

"Her testimony, then."

"She's not credible."

"And he is?"

"In here? No. But out there he's plenty credible. Don't go playing babe in the woods. You know better than anyone how this works."

"What's that supposed to mean?"

"You know what I'm saying. But, you want it plainer, I'll spell it out. How you think you got here, anyway? How you think you made first grade? Frank was a wrong guy and everyone knew it. You took care of him, and you let us take care of you. You blind to that? That's how you got here, Reese. By getting along, going along. That's why you got this tricky precinct. Upper crust meets underbelly. You seemed right for it, like someone right.

"But I'm not telling you anything you don't know, am I? You can't have believed you caught this case by accident. Not for a minute. Not you, Reese. Boys downtown got big plans for you. Letting you cut your teeth on this one. Figure you for a player. That wrong now? You wrong now, Reese? You a wrong cop? You going rogue on us? Or you want back to your roots? Undercover with the underbelly? That what you want? You like that better? Better fit for you? Busting lowlifes to protect the high life? Being a lowlife? Because that can be arranged. We can put you way down deep."

This was too plain for Reese, too much. She couldn't find words.

"Answer me, Detective. How big a problem you got? Or maybe you're a problem we got to solve? You more like Frank than we thought?"

She still couldn't speak. He'd set too many things in motion, too many things swimming her brain. He'd rearranged all the pieces she'd worked so hard to keep ordered. And Frank. Frank was back. Not the Frank who'd come at her for so many months, but the Frank she'd known before, before they'd become the junky couple they were supposed to be playing. Before they'd begun living the lowlife instead of working it.

Second time around this block for Frank, first time for her. And so she'd hid it, or thought she had. She'd played both sides even then—made him look dirtier to make herself look clean. And she'd thought she'd passed. She'd thought she'd pulled it off. She really hadn't understood that it didn't matter. That the brass didn't care. And now she could see it didn't matter whether she'd been set up from the start—whether they'd put her with Frank as a means to his end, or if it had been just a lucky coincidence. She realized none of that mattered now.

The thing that mattered, the thing that got to her, was how incredibly foolish she felt. So blind and naive. A player—what a sick joke that was. All her torment over her actions that night. How she'd worried whether they'd find out. Bust her down. Send her up. Her guilt for their pat on the back. They'd assumed the worst of her and it had made her one of them. That's why they'd rewarded her. Every single thing slippery, and she'd gone right along.

So now, with everything turned on its head, churning in her head, she wondered if being like Frank made her right. Maybe that was their trouble with him. Maybe being wrong, a wrong guy, a wrong cop, meant you could still tell right from wrong. That you still knew the difference, or cared about the difference. Still thought you could be the difference, make a difference.

Reese sat down because her legs couldn't hold the weight of all this new knowledge.

Harris leaned against the edge of his desk. He spoke softly, gently even, in the sick-sweet tones of someone who has you beat and knows it.

"Drop it, here," he said. "It's going to go away. She's going to go away. No need for you to go with her. No need for that whole mess of yours to get dragged out again. And don't think Santerre won't do that. Don't think he can't do that."

And Reese heard him. She listened, and as she did she glanced out the window, saw Eleanor standing outside the interview-room door. Reese watched as her friend talked to Burns, who'd just now arrived.

Reese had always believed Eleanor'd pulled the strings. That it was her friend who'd made it all go away. And then she'd gone away, made her hasty exit from the DA's office just afterwards. Reese wondered how much Eleanor knew. How much she'd known when and how much she'd thought Reese had known.

"Detective?"

"Well, that's it then," Reese said, slowly getting to her feet, making her way to the door.

"We're clear then?" Harris said.

"All clear," Reese said, her hand on the doorknob—one look back at him before she turned it, before she returned to the still-hushed squad room.

Twenty-eight   Alone in his study, Santerre savored the turn of events. Even he couldn't have contrived such an elegant solution. Oh, it was a bit too easy. But his wife having called the cops on herself more than made up for the simplicity. And she'd proved an able adversary in one remaining way: She'd left Nina to him. A problem he would have to solve alone.

Even last night's disruption had its advantages. Certainly it would've been more efficient to have dispensed with her already. But while that plan had practicality, and even some enjoyable elements, it had lacked substance. What he'd do now would come closer to what he'd always wanted. He'd always imagined he could use Nina as he pleased. He'd always planned to reunite her with his wife for one last tryst. Have her his way, and then be done with it.

The others simply couldn't compare. They couldn't put a finish on it. And this he needed—a glossy shine to the end, in order to end it. And he needed it to end, though he'd never betray or admit this. This need would never be let loose, not even in the confines of his own skull. Not this need, not any need.

Reese had walked right past Tom Burns and Eleanor Coffey, and she'd kept walking. She'd only paused to pass a word to

Miller, asking him to keep an eye on things, on Ingrid. Then she'd walked quickly down to the basement garage. There she managed to get in the car, and start on her way without anyone seeming to notice. But as soon as she pulled out onto Forty-second Street, she found herself snarled in rush-hour traffic.

She inched along with all those other cars headed for the West Side Highway, for Westchester, fighting the urge to turn on the siren. All she needed was to broadcast her exit and then have Harris broadcast it back to Santerre.

Harris had really let loose on her, let so many things loose in her. Everything under wrap, underground, underwater, now untied, unburied, swimming up, still thick with murk, catching in her chest, in her throat.

She struggled to remember what had really happened with Frank. But, what with having done the opposite for so long, this wasn't easy. She looked for the glimpses she'd caught in Harris's office. For so long she'd seen Frank only as he'd been that last night—seen him menacing and threatening, coked up, though even this was a lie. Cracked up, was more like it, and her, too. And cranked up. Nasty combination, those two together—crank and crack. It'd made the two of them a nasty combination, real nasty.

She couldn't remember how it had started, them dipping their hands. She truly couldn't have said when it had started. There was no clear demarcation, but rather a blurring. Like her telling herself coke instead of crank and crack. Like telling herself small fuzzy lies for some small measure of comfort. Dipping their hands—they'd just slipped into it. She'd just slipped into it.

She hadn't told anyone, not even Eleanor. He was dirty,

she was clean. That was the story—the cover, her cover. And then under that one, the cover she'd told herself. The cover she'd made just for herself, hardly realizing she'd done it. The cover she'd slipped under. The one she'd stayed under because, like Ingrid, she'd needed some semblance of warmth. And now Harris had yanked her out from under. And she felt just as cold and alone as she'd always feared she would.

Like Reese, Santerre couldn't have said when it turned. He couldn't have pinpointed the crossing—the precise place where accident had become design. It fell somewhere after Lila. Perhaps it had begun with Nina. His failure with her. Her failing him. Nina wasn't like his daughter, and, so, she wasn't like him. She didn't much like him.

No, Nina was soft on his wife. Lila never was. Lila wasn't soft at all. She was her father's daughter. He smiled slightly at the thought of her. An odd smile, accompanied by an odd sensation. But, of course, feeling anything at all was a rarity for him. He cherished his restraint, considered it his most enviable trait, his greatest strength.

His wife had no restraint. None but that which he imposed. And, just this once, she'd eluded his control, disrupted his plans. No matter. He'd finish it without her. A weaker man, a less practical man might have succumbed to endless postponements. One postponement may have proved unavoidable, even fortuitous. But any further postponement would be indulgent and foolhardy, and he would be neither. Above all else Gabriel Santerre understood the importance of timing.

. . .

Carver knew he'd send for her. Whatever drug he'd given her had finally and fully worn off, leaving her edgy and clear. Her first instinct, as always, was to put herself back under. She pulled a syringe from her drawer, but it was empty. It would have been easy enough to find a full one, or fill this one, but instead she tossed it back. She knew it wouldn't work.

The thing that would do the job? That vial was still clenched in her hand and she wasn't ready to let it go. She wasn't ready to use it. She took it with her to the bathroom, placed it carefully in the medicine chest before she showered. And when she'd finished with her shower, finished drying off, she retrieved it.

She carried it to the bedroom, put it on the dresser, and then she began to get dressed—dressed for him. She accomplished this easily and quickly enough, then started downstairs with the vial once more in her hand. She paused briefly, almost went back for her bag, before deciding she didn't need it, before deciding everything she needed was in the palm of her hand.

Once downstairs in her sitting room—the only room that felt halfway hers—she waited on the couch. And as she waited, she tucked the vial into her stocking, secured it between the tight fabric and her thigh. Then she smoothed her skirt, leaving one hand to rest on the small nugget. If she could not avoid or postpone what was coming, she'd at least be prepared.

Soon she heard tires on the gravel driveway. She went to the door unable to restrain her hope that when she opened it, she'd find Reese on the other side. Instead, there was the limo.

. . .

By now Reese had made it to the highway. The traffic was still thick but at least it was moving. She maneuvered carefully, finding what openings she could. She tried to stay focused on her destination—the only place left in this whole sorry mess where she could still make a difference. But it had already grown dark out, and this only added to her fear that she might well be too little, too late.

Santerre waited in his study. He'd considered drugging Nina again, but decided he could afford to enjoy himself a bit. There'd be no sport in it, no challenge at all, if he resorted to the drug. And he deserved some challenge. He'd given up so much already.

Without the drug to help her, Carver felt unusually lucid, her vision painfully clear. The red glare from the limo's small digital clock distracted and irritated her. She closed her eyes and let her hand rest on her thigh, on the vial still secured beneath her stocking.

The limo pulled into the driveway. And Carver, hearing that familiar sound of tires on gravel, opened her eyes. The car pulled to a stop and Carver got out. She walked to the door. As usual, it was unlocked. She went inside, but she did not lock the door behind her. And, as she crossed the marble hall, as she made her way to the study, she kept her hand on her thigh.

She entered the dimly lit room. Santerre stood at the bar. He said nothing to her, acknowledged her arrival only by offering her a drink. She took it and sat down on the couch. From there, she watched Santerre as he freshened his drink. He'd turned from her to do this and so she watched his back, could see his hand on the glass, then on the ice, then the bottle.

Her hand stayed on her thigh, on her vial. She looked around the room, but her eyes kept darting back to him. Her gaze repeatedly drawn to the one small area he occupied. There the light was strong, yet seemed to have no origin. Light spilled into his glass as if from nowhere, glanced off ice and amber liquid.

Carver shook her head, tried to clear away this peculiar kaleidoscope. She told herself he'd probably had the bar specially lit, that she'd simply never noticed before—always too grogged from the drug. She'd never noticed either that he drank constantly, but never appeared drunk.

Tonight, she would've liked him a little sloppy, a little careless, but she saw none of this. And, though she didn't want to, never wanted to, she thought of Ingrid. Thought of the words Ingrid used to recount the night he'd murdered their daughter. "He lost control. Well, that never quite describes him, but that is what happened. In a way." And it had been happening ever since. And Ingrid had let it. Carver had let it.

Now, though she watched him carefully, his turning toward her caught her off guard, threw her off balance. Now, he came at her as light—blinding, shattering light, blistering light. Her hand jerked from her thigh as if on its own, shielded her eyes.

She shook her head again, but could not dim or change what she saw, though he could. If he moved from her, he dimmed. If he came closer, he brightened. This was some parlor trick, except Carver feared it wasn't a trick at all. She could feel heat radiating from him, or from inside her. The closer he came, the less she could distinguish between them.

He took her hand. She felt his heat in her palm. Her other hand went reflexively to her thigh. She felt it there—her vial—grounding her, suppressing his charge. Enough to dampen him a bit until he led her into the huge hall. There, he flared up again. The chandelier, the sconces—all these crystal baubles hungry for light, reflected scattered bits of him in all directions. Light glittering from one bit of cut glass then another, skidding across the white marble, disappearing into that black center star, hungry, too.

He dragged her now. She, too, skittered across the marble. Scattered light, all that glass and marble. She tripped, she landed on her knees. A flash of Ingrid that first night curled amongst shattered glass. Carver's hand brushed the small scar on her knee as Santerre hoisted her to her feet. Her hand went again to her vial. He'd taken hold of her arm, employed that familiar, well-placed grasp.

He made their way to the stairs and then worked their way up them. Upstairs, the light narrowed and focused. Carver remembered the red flash in the car, having to shield her eyes from the clock. She wondered if this was some strange form of withdrawal. She couldn't remember ever going without it this long, not having the drug to dull and dim all her senses, make her senseless. Maybe this was overload—all her senses crashing back, all at once. Except they weren't, not all of them, just vision, maybe touch. His hand burned on hers. Her hand burned on the vial.

He opened the bedroom door. No light here at all. Cavernous black, cool and empty just before he dragged her inside. Then, heat and light bounced the walls. He let go of her hand. She turned it palm up, looked for a brand, but saw nothing. Still, she shook it; it still seared and singed. And she knew as well as anyone, better than anyone, that the things that hurt most are most often unseen.

He didn't ask her to undress and she certainly didn't volunteer. Having sex with him in this state of heightened awareness, with any awareness—impossible, simply and starkly impossible. Hell, that's what the drug was about. What it had always been about. That much predated Santerre. That need, that necessity turned trap.

Besides, this had never been about sex. And though Carver'd been slow to admit it, had refused to admit it, anyone on the game learned that fast enough. And the game carried to this extreme? A game like Santerre's, like Ingrid's? The twisted truth in these netherworlds, of these netherworlds? The truth in a place where each and every thing was turned upside down? The truth of such places was that only love mattered, love and the lack of it.

Twenty-nine   Reese had cleared the city limits. She now cruised the highways of Carver's world. She went over her plan again and again until it swam circles around her. Get there, get in, get Carver out, not much more to it than that. What to do, how to do it, this seemed simple and clear. But it left her circling back—back and around an endless loop that started with Frank and ended with Carver, and then began all over again.

Frank had taken her on some trip. She'd really gone to the far reaches with him. And she'd come back alone. Alone and changed, and with everything changed. Hell, she'd only recently learned how much. That she'd gone too far to ever come all the way home. But, still, she'd never quite lived there, and she'd been born someplace else. These things couldn't be said for Carver. Carver'd been born to this. And so while Carver could know Reese, Reese would never know Carver. But she'd come close enough. She'd had a near-enough brush that she wanted to try. She understood enough to care whether Carver lived or died.

The girl who'd started all this—started it again for Reese—she'd stayed on ice the whole time, would remain just another numbered Jane Doe. And Lila, who'd truly begun it—ashes. Cremated before autopsy. How terribly neat and tidy. How businesslike.

Santerre pushed Carver onto the bed. She landed facedown, quickly rolled to her back. He still gleamed. She shook her head once more, then once again. But he still came at her as light, though not blinding. Her eyes must've adjusted because now she could discern things.

Through his shirt she could see his necklace. That vial, the one hanging from his neck, glowed green-yellow, burned brighter than he did. It held her gaze. She stared so intently her eyes burned and teared. A quick movement broke her away. Precisely, deftly, Santerre had removed his belt. Now he brandished it, snapped it once, then twice between his hands. This oxblood band, this ribbon of darkness splitting his light, gave Carver focus, fixed her gaze.

She crept away from him. And, as she did, she could hear him laughing at her. But she did not look. She would not look at him. She knew not to. She looked only at the belt, rested her eyes in its dusky quiet while she calculated his progress toward her, her progress away. This once she would act as precisely as he did.

She waited for the moment, that instant when he'd have to kneel on the bed to come any closer. She'd backed against the headboard, had no farther to go. He still came at her. Unhurried and assured, he came at her. And, one hand still on her vial, she waited for him. She waited until he had one knee on the bed and the other in motion, and then she sprang at him.

Carver grabbed the belt with both hands and held fast. She could hear Santerre's laughter growing louder and louder. He pulled and she pulled. And the harder she pulled the louder he laughed. Then a sharp beat of quiet, one long studied pause, and he let go.

Carver hurtled back. She crashed to the bed as his laughter boomed all around her. And then he spoke. Quietly, almost wistfully, he said, "Ah, Nina, I'm going to miss these little games of yours."

He'd nearly slipped the belt from her startled fingers, but his words, his calling her by that name, snapped her back and she grabbed the belt from him again.

Santerre tussled with Carver. He admired her fight, indulged her even, relishing the sport of it. She'd proved herself a more able adversary than he'd ever imagined. But enough was enough. He had business to finish. He'd begun to tire of this game.

Carver again weighed and waited. She still grappled with the belt, but she, too, was playing. Now she turned his trick back on him. She dropped the belt, gaining a moment's distraction as he fell slightly off-balance and away. She palmed her vial, then went for his pants pocket, for the vial she knew he had tucked inside it.

Santerre felt her hand grasping his pocket. Her trying to pull herself up by it. Well, he'd squash that. His belt now firmly in hand he pulled away forcefully, once and for all. But when he did, the sound of fabric tearing split his ears. He raised up, gazed down at his ruined pants, and then he raised his hand in rage.

Carver could see it coming. She made one last attempt to work his dismembered pocket. Her eyes never left his hand. Her hand never left his pocket. She kept at it, pressing her vial in, slipping his vial out. But just when she'd thought she'd done it, the pocket tore completely. The useless piece of cloth spilled both vials to the bed.

Santerre reared up again. His fury so consuming one would think she'd torn flesh and not some bit of cloth. His fury so blind as to obscure the two vials, or at least Carver hoped so. She didn't have time for more than hope. He'd raised his hand higher, would bring it down harder. She kept one eye on Santerre, the other on the vials. The last of their scuffling sent one of the two to the floor.

Now, the only vial she saw was the one dangling from his neck. The last thing she saw, still gleaming and glowing. One last bit of light before his hand came down, before everything went dark.

Reese drove the dirt roads in frustrated fury. In her haste, she'd missed turns. She'd had to retrace her way through this godforsaken labyrinth. And everything so quiet out here, always so quiet, she still felt like the marauding intruder.

But at last she found it. She tore up Santerre's long graveled driveway, skidded to a halt between the limo and the door. Gun drawn, she leapt from the car. First she saw the limo driver. He came toward her looking more curious than menacing. But Reese wasted no time making such distinctions. She trained her gun on him. His hands went up instantly. Obligingly, he let her handcuff him to the wrought-iron railing that decorated the door. She gagged him, too, though he'd yet to make a sound.

The next obstacle was the door, but like the driver, it easily complied. Reese hit the hallway in a mad dash. She nearly lost her balance as her shoes hit all that pretty marble. Her near-fall cautioned her. She forced herself to slow down, evaluate, regain some stealth.

She glanced around, discerning what she could in the dim, flickering light. The path seemed clear enough. She simply followed the lights, let the sconces lead her up the stairs. At the head of the stairs eerie light crept from a door left slightly ajar. She paused just outside it, took a deep breath. With this slight motion, she'd brushed one of the sconces. A faint tinkling began as crystals gently collided. It was the only sound Reese could hear. No other sound or sign of life.

Both hands on her gun, she used her foot to edge open the door. Next to no light in here—little glints in sickly hues, blue-greens, greenish yellows, bruised colors. A moment before Reese's eyes adjusted, and then she saw her—saw Carver strung up. The oxblood belt strong and snug against her pale, blue neck. Reese forced herself through slow, deliberate motions, quelled her urge to run to the girl.

Arms outstretched, gun still tightly clenched in both hands, she swept her path. Still he surprised her, coming from shadows, quickly moving, yet not seeming to stir—a glint of clean silver, his cuff links, her first inkling. And then his voice, sounding sickly, blue.

"Ah," he said wearily, "the lady detective. I expected you a bit earlier. A shame you didn't arrive a bit earlier."

It was all he said and she said nothing in return. As he moved closer she could see that aside from his crisp cuffs, his clothing was rumpled, disheveled. Her eyes followed his hand as it reached into his nonexistent pocket. He twisted the small bit of fabric in his hand. He looked almost boyish, childlike—his shirt half-tucked, his collar open, his tie undone and askew, and the grin on his face more sheepish than smug.

Reese realized he wasn't moving toward her, but toward the bed. She kept moving there, too. She tried to edge closer, edge him away. But he simply ignored her. He sat down on the bed, jostling Carver.

"Mr. Santerre, get up and move away from the bed."

But now he was back. Now he chuckled. That same sound she remembered so clearly from their first encounter.

"Mr. Santerre," she repeated, louder this time, "up and off that bed now."

"Or what?" he asked. "You're not going to shoot me, Detective. We both know this. Won't bring this one back," he said, giving Carver a light shove. It sent her body slightly rocking. "Won't bring back your two others. I've got your body count right, don't I, Caroline? May I call you Caroline?"

He reached for his nonexistent pocket again, then moved on—took a vial from the bed.

He opened the vial and dumped the contents across the glass-topped bedside table. Reese felt a familiar, queasy flutter. There was a lot of it there. No doubt pharmaceutical. Santerre extracted his penknife and gold tube from his other, still-intact pocket. He placed the tube beside the powder. Then he opened the knife, began fashioning extravagant portions in neat geometric designs.

Reese tried to unlock her gaze. But Santerre, having finished his sculpting, took up the tube and bent toward the closest, most intricate pattern. But then he stopped and turned to her, said, "Where on earth are my manners?"

He held the tube toward her. "Ladies first," he said, and when she balked he said, "Come, come, now, Detective. Caroline. I believe you acquired quite a taste for this. With that partner of yours. What was his name? Now, don't tell me, I'll get it. Frank. Yes, that was it, Frank. Frank Thompson. Good man as I understand it. Very helpful, until . . . Well, I don't need to tell you he went sour. And I certainly don't need to remind you of his unfortunate demise."

And so another piece fell into place. All along Santerre had possessed this knowledge. He'd simply been waiting to use it while Reese had busied herself with disconnected pieces to avoid the big picture. Carver's words in her head, "Work so different down here?" She forced her gaze off the drug. Her eyes darted to Carver's gently rocking body. Reese's stomach turned, she looked away, briefly met Santerre's eyes before dropping her gaze. For the first time she noticed the chain around his neck—that vial with its green-yellow fluid.

Without knowing its contents, her stomach turned yet again, while her mind raced back to the morgue. Her feet on that squeaky clean floor, smelling that smell, pulling that solid, satisfying latch. Then pulling that tray. This time, Carver inside that bag.

"My dear, you look like you've seen a ghost."

His voice startled and sharpened her. She looked away from the vial and put her eyes to the floor. There she saw another vial lying near his shoe.

"Well, if you're not going to join me, you won't mind if I go on without you."

She kept staring at the floor, could hear his snorting. The intermittent sound went on and on, while she just kept staring at his feet. The gun hanging from her hand, useless in her hand.

Santerre had finished apparently. The snorting sounds had stopped. He said, "I expect it's time I phoned the local authorities." He had the receiver in his hand, but then paused, said, "Will it cause you embarrassment to be discovered here? I assume we understand each other now. I could simply . . ."

The words hung there. Reese looked up as Santerre lurched forward and down. He hit the floor on hands and knees, gasping, trying to crawl.

Reese darted for Carver. She snatched Santerre's knife from the table and sawed through his belt. When Reese had freed her neck and wrists, Carver fell limp. Reese felt Carver's throat—a pulse there, Reese was sure of it. She began quickly force-feeding air, but nothing happened. Still, she kept at her and at her. She heard sputters, stopped momentarily before she realized they came from Santerre.

She slapped Carver hard, back and forth across her face, clasped her head again, had hold of her hair. Then a quick, heavy blow blindsided Reese. It clipped the side of her head with enough force to throw her off Carver. As Reese rolled, she felt for her gun, cradled it as she came up to face him. But another blow sent her back down, then another. Fierce, frenzied blows slammed her again and again.

She'd raised her gun, aiming before she'd sighted her mark. Nearly shot blind, but then she saw, saw it was Carver. Her eyes wide open, but wild—unseeing and glazed. "Stop it," Reese yelled at her. Carver's head snapped up, then left to right, shaking, all of her shaking as she recognized Reese.

The detective stole a look at Santerre. He still crawled

the floor, but kept falling, clutching his stomach and writhing. Reese looked at Carver, then back at Santerre, back and forth, back and forth until she grew dizzy.

A sound filtered through, starting faint, growing louder—an incessant mechanical chirping. A man's voice broke through. Reese looked at Carver, and Carver at Reese, as the voice droned robotically. "Please hang up. There appears to be a receiver off the hook. Please check your main telephone and extension and then try your call again. Thank you. This is a recording."

Now both Carver and Reese stared at the receiver, still dangling from the bedside table. The recording began again, only to be cut short by that hideous mechanized mewling. It mingled with Santerre's strangled whimpers. Reese started to get up, but Carver grabbed her arm. "It'll stop," she said. "If we give it time, it'll stop."

Reese looked from the receiver to Carver.

Carver now stared at Santerre. "If we wait, it'll stop."

Reese pulled free of her. She picked up the receiver and returned it to its cradle. As she did, she noticed the remnants of the drug.

Carver said, "Should be enough, if we give it time."

Reese traced a finger across the tabletop, then tasted the residue—not cocaine, but heroin. She turned to Carver.

"You . . . ?" she said, but went no further than this before trailing off, before sliding into a chair—a satin-covered one, beside the nightstand, just on the other side of the nightstand. From there Reese waited. And she watched, watched Carver as Carver kept watch over Santerre. And Reese tried. She tried very hard not to think or feel anything.

SATURDAY

Thirty   They kept vigil until dawn, until the first traces of sunlight crept through the bedroom windows, until the last traces of breath left Santerre's body. They inspected him together. Reese knelt beside him, felt his throat this time, let her fingers linger until she could be completely sure she felt nothing there. And she herself felt nothing, felt dead inside and out.

As Reese rose to her feet, Carver nudged Santerre with her foot, rolled him onto his back. Now Carver knelt beside him, took firm hold of the chain and the vial. She yanked hard and the necklace gave way. In response to Reese's questioning look, she said simply, "It's mine."

They went downstairs together. Opened the door to find Tony still there, waiting patiently, if uncomfortably—still bound and gagged. Reese unlocked the cuffs, loosened the gag. She said, "You don't work here anymore. You understand me?"

He nodded.

"You got your own car?"

Another nod.

"Get in it, and drive, and then drive some more. We understand each other?"

One more nod, and he was gone.

Reese followed Carver back into the house, followed her

to Santerre's study. Soon after, they heard a car barreling away. "That take care of him?" Reese asked.

Carver nodded, then said, "He's all right. He'll know what to do."

And for the first time in a long while, Reese thought of Ingrid. Heard the woman's words in her head. "Nina's all right . . . She can take care of herself. She made that plain, didn't she? She didn't need me." So many of Ingrid's words etched in Reese's memory. These ones she could only now begin to understand. Carver'd taken care of it all. She hadn't needed Reese. It would've come out the same.

But just then Carver said, "Thank you."

Reese said, "What the hell for?"

"You hadn't come when you did, I'd be dead. If you hadn't come in the first place, I'd've been dead that much sooner."

Reese looked at her blankly.

The girl said, "Don't you get it? You still don't get it?"

Reese shook her head.

"I bought that for me, not for him. I saved it for me. Don't you see?"

Reese was beginning to, though she wasn't sure she wanted to. Kill or be killed. Kill yourself or be killed. These were choices. These were the choices. Ones she and Carver had made. And justice—when it wasn't up for sale, it was up for grabs. They'd simply snatched a small piece of it. They'd beaten Santerre at his game.

"I'd better call it in," Reese said. "Be better if you're not here, haven't been here. How well they know you?"

"Can't say. But if it wasn't your people telling him where I'd been it was these ones. Probably both. He always worked both sides. Always liked a neatly stacked deck."

"Okay, I don't want to put you at your place. So, I guess that leaves my car. Your choice—floor or trunk?"

"Nobody's putting me in a trunk."

"All right, then. Floor is it, but head down and covered. And we need to get what's left of that belt. Anything else put you here? Where's your bag?"

"Home."

"Okay, so let's get the belt and get this over."

They climbed the stairs to the bedroom. Santerre lay just where they'd left him. Reese gathered the remnants of the belt, finding Santerre's knife among them. She wiped it clean, then went to his body, pressed his hand to it. Had she touched anything else that mattered? The phone, but that was okay. That could be explained. Besides, with him dead she figured no one would want too much explaining.

They returned to the study. Reese used the phone atop the man's massive desk. Conveniently, fittingly, the local cops still ranked number one on Santerre's speed-dial. She pressed the key, then leaned against the heavy wood. The town's sleepy desk sergeant answered. She'd wanted this, wanted to call early enough to catch the tail end of the night shift. "There's been an accident," she said. "Gabriel Santerre's house. Yes. Mr. Santerre is dead. Reese, detective, NYPD. That's right. Yeah, yeah, send everything you got."

She hung up, looked at Carver, and said, "Let's get you into that car."

They went outside. Reese stashed the bits of belt in the glove compartment, then moved her car to a less conspicuous locale, hid Carver in the back, under a blanket. She looked around. The limo didn't look great where it was, but moving it'd be worse. She'd play dumb on that front. And she was sickly sure they wouldn't ask. Only one reason a man like Santerre got loyalty and that reason didn't exist if he didn't. No, they'd be more concerned with covering up— protecting and serving themselves.

She could already hear the sirens. And soon the caravan raced up the driveway: an unmarked car, three squad cars, one EMS truck—they all pulled up around her.

One man, plainclothes, approached her. The rest waited beside their various vehicles in their various uniforms.

"You call it in? You Reese?" this one asked, still walking toward her.

"Yep," she said, as he came to a stop. "And you're?"

"Marks, Detective Marks. Any idea what happened?"

He'd started amiably enough, so she followed his lead. "Looks like overdose," she said calmly. "Drug paraphernalia and such near the body."

"And you're out here . . . ?"

"Investigating that homicide. Had some questions for Mr. Santerre. The hotel thing, but I guess you've heard all about that."

"Can't say I have."

"Oh." If he wanted to play dumb, she'd let him, assuming he'd extend her the same courtesy.

"And he's?"

"Upstairs."

"Dead."

"Very."

"Guess I better send my boys in." He waved his hand and all the uniforms headed for the door. "Guess I better get on in there myself. Say, how'd you get in?"

"Door was open. Guess you keep it pretty safe out here for a man like Santerre . . ."

"How's that?"

"For a man like Santerre, you know, to leave his door unlocked. Guess he had a lot of confidence in you all."

"Well, I couldn't really say."

And so it went—both of them baiting hooks and casting lines. Neither of them biting. Neither one really wanting to catch anything.

Reese said, "You want me to stick around?"

"Naw, we'll take it from here. You're Midtown, right?"

"Uh-huh," she said, knowing he knew this because of the case she worked. The one he claimed to know nothing about.

"So," he said, "I know where to find you."

Marks headed for the house, while Reese headed for her car. That'd sure gone smooth. She hoped not too smooth. Though she still knew her first instinct was the right one, the one to trust. She wasn't going to start second-guessing now. No, the locals just wanted her gone so they could do their own cleanup. Take care of business. She'd dropped enough hints. They'd want her kept out of it, far and away.

She figured it'd work the same way at her own house. With the hold on Harris eliminated, so went the lieutenant's hold on her. This solution went way beyond Carver's interests. It'd solve a lot of problems up and down the line—the public and private chain of command. Until the next Santerre came to power. The king is dead. Long live the king. Hardly a new story.

One last look at the house, and then she got into her car. "Stay down and quiet till I tell you different," she said. And then she drove away. She simply drove away.

Thirty-one   Reese didn't speak until they'd cleared the dirt-road maze and the rural routes. They were well on their way, on the highway, heading south, when she said, "Okay."

Carver threw off the blanket. She climbed over and into the front seat just like a child would. Reese glanced at her. She looked shaken and worn and, yes, a bit childlike. Like she was looking for something, something from Reese. Unsure what else to offer, the detective held out her hand. Carver took it, then said quietly, "Do you think it's over? Really over?"

"Yes."

"What'll happen to her? To Ingrid?"

"I don't know. She killed that girl. She admitted it."

"I know."

"You do?"

"He told me."

"When?"

"Last night. Or, no, this was last night. The night before."

"He told you what?"

"That she drowned. The girl, that she drowned her. Ingrid did. That he'd make sure she confessed. Or, actually, he said you would. That you'd take care of his wife for him. That he'd take care of me. He would've that night, except for a phone call."

"Lucky timing."

Reese said it flatly, wanted Carver to leave it alone for now. The girl complied, leaving Reese alone with her thoughts, this extra piece. He had gotten the report early, though it didn't surprise her. Nothing much had the capacity to surprise her anymore, not where Santerre was concerned.

And Ingrid? Well, let the wheels turn. Let the wheels crush her. Let them carry her away until the end of time, for all Reese cared. She wondered if the woman already knew about her husband. She relished the idea of delivering the news. Though if the woman didn't know she was certainly the only ignorant one left in Midtown.

Reese glanced at Carver again. Questioned the wisdom of taking her back with her. But decided it wouldn't matter. Better than leaving her at that house of hers. The locals might still take a crack at her. Reese couldn't be sure how that crew might play. Where Carver might fit into their cleanup. Carver'd know the answer to this better than Reese would. She'd played this game for years. She'd sure shown Reese. Carver'd shown just how practiced and seasoned she was—a real player.

Maybe Reese was a player now, too, after all. Squeezed this tight for this long, was there any other way out? But if she was, she wasn't the player Harris had expected. The one Santerre had expected, made to order, to follow his orders. Hell, she wasn't even playing the same game. Or was she? From a different side, a different angle—was there any difference? Had she made any difference?

Carver'd said she had. But Carver didn't know about those moments Reese had stood spellbound—gripped by Santerre, unable to free herself from his hold. Carver'd freed her before she'd freed Carver.

She stole another look at the girl. "You want to see her again? Ingrid, I mean? You need that?" Reese asked now.

"Think she knows?"

"Not sure."

"What's your guess?"

"They've left her to me. But that's not the same as her not knowing. Word travels pretty fast down there, especially down in the cells."

"I want to be there. I want to see her face."

"Okay, then."

They'd hit the city limits, and then the city itself. Reese cruised down the West Side Highway, then across Forty-second Street. As they neared the station house, Reese said, "Better get that belt out of the glove box."

Carver opened it, took the pieces. They felt hot in her hands, but then the heater had been blasting the whole way. She knew that's what caused it, all it was.

"You want 'em, they're yours," Reese said.

"No, I've got what's mine."

"Yeah, you want to tell me what that was?"

"The piece of me he kept. But these, these are yours."

Carver handed them over, and Reese slipped them into her coat pocket. Then she'd turned into the station house, and there they were, once again in that garage. And again, Reese led Carver in through the back.

As soon as they were in, the buzz was audible, palpable, growing louder with each flight of stairs. And each person or cluster they passed went silent and stared. Reese glared. Word had traveled, all right—fast and for sure.

Reese tempered herself just a little, just outside the

squad room. And then in they went, faced off more silent stares. Reese felt herself sneer. No one would take point on this one, no one in this room. They'd all wait for Harris.

They didn't have to wait long. His door swung open. He said, "Reese, in here."

She took measured steps, still with Carver in tow. She would not hurry. She crossed the room, letting them all watch and wonder. Harris's tone so neutral, it gave them no clear path to follow.

Once inside her lieutenant's office, Reese took command. "Has Mrs. Santerre been informed?" she asked before Harris could speak.

"No, Detective, you know we save her . . ."

"I'd like her brought up now."

"First, you want to bring me up to speed, Detective. Privately."

"Oh, I don't think there's anything you haven't heard by now, Lieutenant."

"How's about we have a little private talk, anyway, without your friend. I don't believe we've even been introduced."

"I need to inform Mrs. Santerre. This young woman is a friend of the family."

"I see," Harris said, reaching for the phone. He gave Reese a long studied gaze before hitting a few keys, then he spoke evenly into the air. "Have Mrs. Santerre brought up to interview three . . ."

Reese, interrupting, said, "I want room two."

"Hold on that," Harris said, flicking off the speaker.

Again Reese spoke before he could. "This is a private matter. We have no need, no right, to monitor it."

"Have you forgotten the woman confessed to murder?"

"That has no bearing on this, and you know it."

Harris flicked the speaker again. "Make it two," he said, and clicked off without waiting for a reply.

Reese had won another round. Apparently Harris hadn't received word on how this thing would shake out. And he didn't appear ready to decide for himself.

"Okay, you got what you want. Tell the wife, but then you're going to tell me."

"Whatever you say, Lieutenant."

The squad room's hum suddenly notched up. It approached a din now, signaling Mrs. Santerre's arrival. Reese took her cue, and took Carver. The three women were soon behind closed doors—alone and in quiet. A quiet that Ingrid immediately shattered. "What's happened?" she asked, her voice both fierce and trembly. "What's happened to my husband?"

Reese spoke so slowly, she nearly drawled. "Your husband's dead, Mrs. Santerre."

"But how?"

"An accident." Reese stretched the last word, delivered it long and gangly, let it hang.

"What kind of accident?"

"Drug overdose, apparently," Reese said, now speaking crisply, efficiently. "Heroin."

"But my husband doesn't take heroin." Then Ingrid looked at Carver, and said, "You . . . You were there."

Carver simply nodded.

"My God," Ingrid said. She looked from Carver to Reese and then back again.

A knock on the door disrupted this cozy moment. Reese went to answer it, finding Miller there. She kept her guard up even for him. "Yes?" she said evenly.

"I got Eleanor on the phone. What should I tell her?"

Reese looked back at the two women. She decided to give Carver and Ingrid a little time on their own, figured she owed that to Carver. "I'll talk to her," Reese said. "But you plant yourself here. No one gets in. No one gets out."

Behind the door Miller now guarded, Ingrid and Carver still stared at each other. "My God," Ingrid said again. "Did you think that's what I wanted? Did you do it for me?"

"Oh, spare me. But you can't, can you? Not me, not anyone. Neither of us would be here now if you could. Can you not for a second think of someone 'sides yourself?"

"Nina, darling, please . . ."

"That's not my name, and that's not going to work. You got nothing to say for yourself. Nothing to say to me. Not now, not ever. We understand each other? We finally understand each other?"

Carver'd reduced the woman to mute nods. Ingrid sat there still—still and quiet.

Reese came back into the room, looked at Carver, and said, "You finished, here?"

"Yes, absolutely."

And so they left. They left Ingrid to fend for herself. They left the station house. Reese didn't care—let them think whatever they wanted. And let Harris wait. And he would wait. If he didn't know how this would come down, she did. And she knew she'd come out all right. She'd shown them a side of herself they wouldn't want to see, but couldn't ignore. She'd shown she could play. She'd shown she could win. No matter how much shuffling they did, it'd come out the same. She'd still hold all the cards.

Thirty-two   Out on the sidewalk Reese asked Carver, "You want some coffee, or something? Something warm?" The girl'd been shaking on and off now for hours.

"A drink's what I need. It'll hold it off a bit."

Reese had almost forgotten. "How long you gone?"

"A day, maybe two. A drink and a trip to the bank ought to do it. I want to get my money and get gone."

They bought a pint of vodka, and then Reese hailed a cab. Carver gave the address—Madison Avenue in the Sixties. They passed the bottle back and forth until the cab pulled up at one of those Upper East Side private banks, one in a town house, no less. Reese started to get out with her, but Carver stopped her, said, "Look, this is where I get off."

"But what'll you do? Where will you go?"

"First, in there. Then anywhere I want. My job's done, Detective. Isn't yours?"

"Just about," Reese said.

Then Carver began pulling away, was almost out of the cab before she turned back one last time. She gave Reese a hurried hug, and something resembling a kiss on the cheek. Then she left Reese. Left Reese to watch her disappear, watch her vanish through the doors of the brownstone.

"Meter's running, lady. You want another stop, or what?"

Reese gave the cabbie Eleanor's address.

As Reese's cab made its way farther uptown, Carver was escorted to her safe-deposit box. From it she extracted bundles of cash, her passport, and her passbook—her Swiss one. These things she put into a heavy canvas bag the bank provided.

Into the now empty box, she dropped the vial and chain. She relished the sound, the satisfying echo of glass and chain hitting metal. Then she shut the box, hoisted it, and shoved it back into the wall.

Back out on Madison, she went to the nearest of the many stores and bought a bag. She put her canvas bag inside this new one. Soon she was in her own cab, bound for Kennedy Airport's international terminal.

Reese's cab dropped her outside Eleanor's building. This was the last of it for Reese. The last piece that mattered. Reese had kept their earlier phone call crisp. She'd taken only enough time to arrange this meeting. She waltzed past the doorman to the elevator. And, though she'd arrived early, she knew Eleanor waited upstairs.

The elevator opened onto the familiar foyer. Reese gave that lone door a few sharp knocks. She heard footsteps, then the door opened. Her friend stood, still half-behind the door, with a wary look on her face, or a worried one.

"Is it true?" Eleanor asked, ushering Reese inside.

"What?"

"Santerre's dead? You were out there? Is that all true?"

"Yes."

"But there's more, isn't there?"

"Yes."

"So tell me."

"You first."

"What?"

"You're going to tell me some things first, about Frank. About what you knew when. What you thought you were doing. Thought I was doing. Then we'll see what I tell you."

"Caroline . . ."

"No, we're going to do this and do it now."

"What's happened? Did Harris . . . ?"

"Oh, yes, Harris. He got pretty blunt. Told me just about everything but your part in it. Where you fit. You want to tell me? Or you want me to guess?"

"Hey, I left."

"Yeah, I know. Now tell me why, and tell it fresh."

"I left when I couldn't take it anymore. What it was doing to me. What they were doing to you . . ."

"And what exactly was that?"

"Look, I still don't know if they set you up. If they put you under with Frank, hoping for a certain result."

"A certain result. That's what you call it these days?"

"Caroline, I didn't know what they were up to any better than you did."

"But you knew sooner . . ."

"Only because you wouldn't see it. I tried a hundred different ways and times to tell you, but would you listen? Could you hear it? No. You just kept moving forward, blind and deaf to what had passed. To what was going on all around you. The way they were moving you around.

"Caroline, I moved on because you gave me no other

choice. How many times I had to listen to you agonize. You killed the man they wanted dead and they paid you handsomely for it. And ever since, you been paying for that payment. Inside. In a way they know nothing about, because they don't work that way. You still work that way? Which way you work now? Which way you going to work it, now you can finally see it? Huh, tell me that, why don't you?"

"Maybe I won't work it. Maybe it's time I left, too."

"You know you won't. If you were ever going to do that, you'd've already done it. You'll work it your way. And you'll work better with your eyes open. Aren't you already?"

"Huh?"

"Santerre. Looks like you worked that pretty good. Nobody going to grieve for that man. Not even you."

Reese heard this. She heard all of it. This time she listened. And as she listened, she shoved her hand deep into her coat pocket. Now, she fingered the pieces of leather there. And weighing those pieces against the weight of Eleanor's words, Reese began to balance the scales.

Acknowledgments

The author would like to thank Ann Rower for the grasp and the grapple—for hoisting the wreckage.

Thanks also to: Meredith Carr, Allan Gurganus, Gloria Carol, Mark Ameen, James Baker, and Jane Perkins for consistent support during turbulent times; Dale Peck for his generosity in a pinch and daily; Syd Straw for the exchange of inspiration; Morton L. Janklow and Tina Bennett for more than can be explained; Nan A. Talese, a rare publisher and real editor; and Jesse Cohen for his editorial skill and patience, and for coming up with a title when no one else could.

The Hit
Denise Ryan

The most compelling debut since Martina Cole's

To the world, Shannon's father-in-law is a pillar of the Liverpool community. Only she suspects that Bernard is the monster responsible for raping and murdering a local girl.

No one, including Shannon's CID detective husband, believes the head teacher capable of the horrific crimes she accuses him of. The only person who takes her allegations seriously is Bernard himself – and he decides it's time to silence his troublesome daughter-in-law for good.

Terrified for her life, Shannon realises there's only one way to stop herself becoming Bernard's next victim. It isn't legal. It isn't moral. But it's certainly permanent!

The Trials of Nikki Hill

Christopher Darden and Dick Lochte

It's set to be the most sensational murder trial in L.A. since O.J. Simpson's!

When T.V. presenter Madeline Gray's body is found dumped in gangland Los Angeles, the police immediately have a suspect – Jamal Deschamps, a young black man arrested at the scene with Madeline's ring in his pocket.

For Nikki Hill, an ambitious African-American prosecuting attorney, it's make or break time. Having laboured away in obscurity for years, Deschamps' trial is her chance to prove herself.

Only her supposedly airtight case is springing some big-time leaks, sending Nikki and the L.A.P.D.'s homicide division scrambling to find the real killer, while an army of attorneys, spin-doctors, crooked cops and hardened gangsters starts working overtime to make the wheels of justice spin just the way they want ...

A street-smart legal thriller from Christopher Darden, renowned O.J. Simpson prosecutor, and acclaimed mystery writer Dick Lochte.

"A swift, entertaining read."   *The Washington Post*

"Entertaining...convincing...Darden has delivered one heck of a closing."   ***People***

The very best of Piatkus fiction is now available in paperback as well as hardcover. Piatkus paperbacks, where *every* book is special.

☐	0 7499 3142 6	The Trials of Nikki Hill	Christopher Darden & Dick Lochte	£5.99
☐	0 7499 3140 X	The Hit	Denise Ryan	£5.99
☐	0 7499 3070 5	Denial	Keith Ablow	£5.99
☐	0 7499 3035 7	Haven	John R. Maxim	£5.99
☐	0 7499 3109 4	Little Triggers	Martyn Waites	£5.99
☐	0 7499 3115 9	Blood Red Sky	Neil Gibb	£5.99
☐	0 7499 3101 9	Smoker	Greg Rucka	£5.99

The prices shown above were correct at the time of going to press. However, Piatkus Books reserve the right to show new retail prices on covers which may differ from those previously advertised in the text or elsewhere.

Piatkus Books will be available from your bookshop or newsagent, or can be ordered from the following address:
Piatkus Paperbacks, PO Box 11, Falmouth, TR10 9EN
Alternatively you can fax your order to this address on 01326 374 888 or e-mail us at books@barni.avel.co.uk

Payments can be made as follows: Sterling cheque, Eurocheque, postal order (payable to Piatkus Books) or by credit card, Visa/Mastercard. Do not send cash or currency. UK and B.F.P.O. customers should allow £1.00 postage and packing for the first book, 50p for the second and 30p for each additional book ordered to a maximum of £3.00 (7 books plus).

Overseas customers, including Eire, allow £2.00 for postage and packing for the first book, plus £1.00 for the second and 50p for each subsequent title ordered.

NAME (block letters)_____

ADDRESS _____

_____

I enclose my remittance for £_____

I wish to pay by Visa/Mastercard   Expiry Date:_____
